CHRISTMAS IN TUSCANY

LEGACY SERIES
BOOK 11

PAULA KAY

CONTENTS

ONE

Isabella smiled as she watched her daughter from across the room, her thick dark curls wild and framing the most beautiful face that Isabella had ever known.

Arianna.

The day that Isabella had married Thomas had been the happiest day of her life—until the day she'd given birth to their daughter. Three-year-old Arianna seemed to have them both wrapped around her little finger but she had such a sweet way about her—a disposition that made her a delight to be around.

"Arianna, honey? Are you sharing with the girls?"

Jemma's twins, Chloe and Daisy, seemed to be waiting patiently at the small table, while Arianna stood beside them with her tray of cookies.

"Mommy!" Arianna turned toward Isabella, her forehead creased. "I'm only trying to find the very best cookies for them. They aren't all the same, you know—and Daisy doesn't like the ones with nuts."

Isabella laughed and looked at Jemma, who was grinning beside her on the sofa where Isabella sat opening a big box of

Christmas ornaments. "Okay, honey. When you three finish your tea party, we're going to start decorating the tree, so don't go running off."

"We won't, Mommy."

Isabella placed her hand on her stomach as she felt the sharp kick from inside her. "Listen here, you little soccer player, don't get any wild ideas."

Jemma reached out to touch her arm. "Are you feeling okay? I can handle the three little *amigas* if you want to go lie down for a little bit."

"Thanks, Jem. I'm fine. I'm just not at all sure if this little guy of ours is going to wait until after Christmas to make his appearance. On the one hand, the closer to the due date the better; on the other, I feel as big as a house and my ankles might never be normal again, so you know—maybe get this child out of me already."

Both women laughed and Thomas entered the room, crossing it in quick even strides to sit down beside Isabella and pull her in for a hug, barely fitting his arm around her very large stomach.

"Oh, man. Be careful there, mister. I don't want to squish you." Isabella laughed and allowed herself to close her eyes and relax against the broad chest that had become home to her.

She felt Arianna's presence next to her, before she opened her eyes to see her daughter standing beside them, her little hands on her hips, studying them carefully.

"Mommy, please don't squish Daddy."

Thomas laughed. "Don't worry, honey. Daddy is too strong to be taken down so easily."

Arianna did not look convinced. "Daddy, look how big Mommy's tummy is."

Isabella laughed and sat up so that Thomas could pull Arianna up into his lap, his kisses smothering her face as she giggled, filling the room with the sound that brought them endless joy.

"Daddy, stop. Please." Arianna quieted herself enough to get the words out and then gently placed her head on Isabella's lap, turning her face toward Isabella's stomach. "Hello, little brother."

Isabella ran her fingers over her daughter's hair, careful not to get caught up in the tangles. She felt that overwhelming surge of love—the kind that seemed to literally make her heart beat faster. She'd never known love like the love she had for her daughter. Was it even possible that she could love their son— that they could love their son—even half as much? Everyone assured her that it was true about the depth of love for a child knowing no bounds—that their love would only expand as their family expanded.

She leaned down to kiss Arianna on the head. "Can you feel those kicks? I think your baby brother knows your voice, sweet girl."

Arianna sat up and put her hand gently on Isabella's stomach and then giggled. "I do, Mommy! I do feel him kicking. I wish he would come out soon."

Isabella looked at Thomas and then put her hand in his that reached for her. "I do too, honey. Any day now he's going to make his appearance."

Arianna kissed first Isabella on the lips and then reached for Thomas with a big hug and a quick kiss. "I have to go play with the twins now. They're waiting very patiently for me."

Thomas laughed and set her down on the floor. "Go ahead then. Have fun and play nice."

Arianna turned as if on cue, hands on her hips, which seemed to be a signature stance of hers lately. "Daddy! Why do you say that? You know I always play nice."

Thomas laughed, as did Isabella.

"Honey, you do play nice. Daddy is only kidding."

Thomas nodded his head and squeezed Isabella's hand as Arianna ran over to where the girls were playing. He pulled Isabella in for a kiss, wrapping his arms tightly around her.

"Ugh—I might not ever be able to get off you, you know," said Isabella.

Thomas kissed her on the nose as he looked into her eyes. "That is not so bad, my love. And have I told you how absolutely gorgeous you look today?"

Isabella smiled, thinking how just a moment earlier, she'd felt not the least bit gorgeous. Somehow Thomas made her feel like the most radiant woman in the room—always—no matter the crowd or circumstances. She always felt special when he looked at her, and after four years of marriage, that feeling of total love and adoration had only grown stronger between them.

"You're too sweet to me." She kissed him back. "Somehow I have to muster the energy to get the decorating done today. I promised the girls, and they can't wait to see the lights on the tree."

"Are you feeling okay, honey?" Thomas looked at his watch. "Maybe I can move my meeting and help you out here."

"No. No, it's okay. I'll be fine and Jemma is here. Maybe I will steal away for a small nap before Lia and Gigi come with lunch. Ooh, that sounds delightful, actually."

Thomas leaned down to kiss her on the neck—in just the

place that he knew drove her crazy. "Maybe I have time to join you for that nap." He winked.

Isabella laughed. "I don't think so, honey. I mean, I really need to try to catch a little sleep." She tilted her head back a little to look at him. "But I'll certainly take a rain check on whatever it is you have in mind."

Her added weight and lack of energy did not keep her from wanting her husband. Thomas had only grown more romantic over the years, something that Isabella never tired of.

He grinned back at her and gently helped her to sit up before rising and reaching for her hands to help her up off the sofa.

"That's a deal. I shouldn't be gone long. Dinner is at Lia's tonight?"

"Yes, Mom and Dad get in around two, I think and—Jemma? What time is the rest of your gang coming?"

"Chase is coming with Kylie this afternoon. Mom has that show in Paris. I think she gets in tomorrow."

"And Rafael?" Thomas asked. "Have you heard from him how things are going?"

Just days earlier there had been an earthquake in Guatemala—one that had affected the orphanage. With Jemma's blessing and the promise to be back before Christmas day, Rafael had gotten a flight out straight after they'd heard the news.

"I spoke with him shortly after he arrived. Things aren't great but they've gotten a lot of help with the rebuilding—at least until they can get something more permanent in place. And no one at the orphanage was hurt, thank God."

Isabella sat down on the sofa next to her best friend, putting her arm around her. Jemma and the twins had come to stay with them the day that Rafael had left, and she knew that her friend had concerns that Rafael might not make it back in time for Christmas. Isabella knew that look on her friend's face. Jemma was worried.

"Are you okay?" Isabella said.

"Yeah. Well, I've texted Rafael a few times this morning and I haven't heard back from him.

Thomas walked over and placed a hand on Jemma's shoulder. "Don't worry, Jem. He'll get back in time."

Jemma smiled. "I know. I'm okay. Really. And the girls love being here."

"And I love having you here—you know that!" Isabella laughed.

"And on that note, my friend... Why don't you go have that nap I heard you mentioning? The girls seem pretty content right now and we can decorate the tree after."

Thomas held his hand out to Isabella and she grabbed it, letting him pull her to her feet.

"Well, I will not say no to that idea. Arianna? Mommy's going to go lie down for a few minutes. You mind Aunt Jemma, okay?"

"Okay, Mommy."

Thomas kissed her on the lips. "Have a nice rest, my darling. I'll see you all later this afternoon. Thanks, Jemma."

Isabella turned back toward Jemma before she made her way upstairs to the bedroom. "Thanks, Jem. I won't be long."

"No worries, Bella. Get a good rest while you can."

TWO

After checking in on the girls, who seemed to be content playing house in one corner of the large family room, Jemma grabbed her phone and flopped down on the sofa. Still no word from Rafael. She bit her bottom lip as she punched in another text asking him if everything was alright. It wasn't like Rafael not to respond right away, and she was trying not to feel nervous about it.

She didn't have another second to think about it before she had an incoming call from her mother.

"Hi, Mom."

"Hi, honey. How's it going there?"

Blu's voice sounded strained to Jemma even in the few words that were spoken, and it was very noisy in the background.

"Everything's good. I'm just hanging out with the girls while Bella has a little nap. How's the show going?"

Blu said something that Jemma couldn't make out.

"Mom, I'm having a hard time hearing you. Can you say that again?"

"Let me step outside for a minute."

Jemma waited the few seconds that it took for the line to grow much quieter.

"Sorry, honey. It's a bit crazy here right now, but things are winding down. I was asking you—honey, have you had the news on? Have you heard from Rafael?"

"No, I haven't and I'd be lying if I said I wasn't getting concerned. I know he's busy there right now but it's just not like him..." Jemma suddenly realized how silent her mom was on the other end of the line. "Mom? What's on the news? Has something else happened?" She felt her heartbeat quicken as she waited for Blu to respond.

"Jem, I'm sure he's fine—"

"Mom, you're scaring me."

Jemma saw Chloe's eyes on her from across the room and attempted to quiet her voice. The last thing she wanted was for the twins to see her upset about Rafael. They'd already expressed their fears that their father was going to be away from them at Christmas. She turned her head slightly so that the girls could no longer read the emotions on her face. "Mom, what is it?"

"Honey, there's been another earthquake—a pretty big one, I'm afraid. But I think it's also affected communications—they said that on the news—that a lot of the phone and Internet might be down now. I'm sure you'll be hearing from him soon that everything is alright."

Jemma felt her breath catch in her throat. She couldn't bear it if anything happened to Rafael. She could hardly remember her life without him and the girls—he just had to be okay. But why wasn't he answering her texts?

"Honey? Are you okay? Is someone there with you now?

Jemma, try not to think the worst. I'm sure you'll hear from him soon."

Jemma took a deep breath in and willed herself to answer. "Yes, I'm okay. I mean, I'm not but I guess I just need to keep trying to get a hold of him. Bella's resting upstairs but Lia and Gigi are due any time for lunch."

"I'm sorry, but they're calling me to come back inside. Please text me as soon as you hear anything, and I'm going to call you back as soon as I'm done here, okay?"

"Okay, don't worry. I'm alright." It was a lie but Jemma didn't want Blu worrying about her when she was right in the middle of a big event.

"I love you, honey. Talk to Bella and the others—tell them what's happened, and I'm sure Douglas can help you find out what's going on."

"Okay, yes, that's a good idea. Bye, Mom."

Jemma felt her daughter's hand on her arm as she hung up the phone.

"What's wrong, Mommy?" It was Chloe, always so sensitive to feelings that were swirling around her. Sometimes Jemma actually wondered if the young girl had some kind of psychic ability—she was often that much in tune to the emotions of others.

"Nothing's wrong, honey. Are you girls almost ready for some lunch?"

"Mommy, don't fib."

Jemma laughed despite her still worried thoughts. "Honey, I'm not fibbing. Why do you say that, silly?"

"I can tell. I can always tell when you're not telling me the complete story."

Jemma leaned in to kiss her daughter on the forehead.

Chloe was repeating the very same words that her father had used with her days earlier when he'd caught her lying about something that had happened between her and Daisy.

"Honey, there's no story to tell. Go tell Daisy and Ari that it's time to clean up now. And I'll go get those delicious sandwiches you helped me make earlier."

"And the fruit salad?"

Jemma smiled. "Yes, I won't forget the fruit salad."

Chloe, seemingly satisfied enough to forget the grilling of her mother for information—for now, anyway—ran off to join the other girls.

Jemma watched her run off and then saw Chloe put her arm around her sister, her worried thoughts momentarily interrupted by the physical love she had for her daughters. Twins. She still marveled at it. It seemed impossible that they'd gone through her whole pregnancy without the knowledge that there were two little girls vying for attention in her womb.

She had panicked only for a second when the doctor had told them the news during the delivery—only for that very brief second, before she saw the tears in Rafael's eyes. He'd leaned down to kiss her, squeezing her hand and telling her that everything was going to be just fine—that two babies were just perfect for their family.

First there was Chloe—a name they'd chosen quite easily—followed by her sister. Jemma had gazed down at her with wonder as Rafael held their firstborn and just like that, the name Daisy had come to her and seemed to suit their little surprise daughter perfectly.

Now that they were four, it seemed that every day Jemma noticed the distinct differences between her daughters. Chloe, the eldest by mere seconds, was always the big sister—slightly bossy, and with a watchful eye that seemed to always be on her sister. She was definitely the more vocal of the two.

Daisy was quieter than her sister, but had an equally loud voice when it came to expressing her displeasure over something. She was intensely loyal, never one to tattle, a trait that Jemma found especially endearing. Daisy could play outside for hours; Jemma would often find her under the big tree outside with a favorite book in her hand. Daisy also loved to paint, and while trying not to be biased, Jemma felt that there was definitely some natural talent there.

Yes, their daughters had brought great pleasure to their lives.

Jemma felt the jolt of panic once again as she looked down at her phone screen. *Raf, please text me.* 12:30. Lia and Gigi would be there in a half hour and Isabella was likely to be up before then. She'd just busy herself with the girls and their lunch and try to put any worrisome thoughts out of her mind.

Rafael would be fine. He'd be home for Christmas just like he'd promised Jemma and the girls. Everything would be fine. Jemma recited the words inside her head as if it was a mantra of positive thoughts she could will into fruition.

THREE

Lia pressed the lid onto the last bowl of food that was to go over to Isabella's. She smiled at Gigi as she entered the room with the bottles of wine Lia had asked her to grab from the cellar.

"Do you think we have enough food here?" Lia asked.

Gigi laughed. "I think Bella is going to be mortified at the amount of food we have here for lunch."

Lia glanced at the bowls of pasta and meat dishes on the counter and laughed too. "Oh, it's not all for lunch. I've been bringing meals over to them these last few days—when they're not coming here for dinner. Bella doesn't say much, but I can see her discomfort lately. I figure it's a small thing that I can do for her."

Gigi nodded as she crossed the room to sit down at the small table, and Lia followed her with the two coffees she'd prepared. How many coffees had she shared in this very place with the woman who had become her best friend over the years?

There, they'd talked about their family, retirement, pregnancies, Lia's cancer scare, and all of the numerous topics that bond two women together. There, Gigi had become a trusted friend and the person that Lia always went to first whenever there was something on her mind.

"Did Douglas tell you what time they were planning to be home today?"

Antonio and Douglas had left early that morning to drive to the coast for a meeting. The two men had started doing some business investments together, and Douglas had become mesmerized by a little restaurant that was for sale. Lia doubted it was something that would be of interest to Antonio. He always said that the restaurant business was one of the most difficult and volatile to manage from afar—and that they had enough on their hands with Lia's restaurant, Thyme. But he was teasing whenever he said that last bit. He knew how much Thyme meant to Lia and that it was her baby to manage—though these days it was pretty hands off, Lia deciding when and how much time she wanted to spend there day to day.

Gigi tapped Lia lightly on the arm.

Lia jerked slightly at the touch, realizing that she hadn't heard a word of what Gigi had been telling her. "I'm sorry. What was that?"

"I was just saying that Douglas told me that they'd be back before dinner."

"Oh, good. I can't wait until everyone arrives. Can you think of anything that's not on our list? I feel like I need to do a bit more shopping—for the kids. Maybe a quick trip to Florence, if you're up for it?"

"Maybe, although Douglas has forbidden me from buying one more thing for the girls." Gigi laughed. "Well, he's joking, of course, but I may have gone a bit overboard this year."

"This year? As opposed to any other year?" Lia laughed, knowing full well that she was just as guilty.

Every year Blu, Jemma, and Bella scolded them for buying too much for the children, and every year they just couldn't seem to resist. It was too much fun to see the look on their young faces, the squeals of delight that filled the house, and the hours of playtime after the presents were open. It was Lia's favorite time of year—the one time that she could count on everyone being there together. And this year there was the added anticipation of Bella's and Thomas's son due just days after Christmas.

Gigi smiled at Lia. "Oh, what fun is Christmas, if we don't get to spoil these great kids of ours? Speaking of which—where's Gabriela? Is she still in school?"

"No, they're on vacation since the middle of last week. She's gone skiing with a friend. They're due back tonight and I'll go to pick her up in the morning." She noticed a funny look on Gigi's face. "She begged and begged me, promising to be back before everyone had gathered. Well, you know that she'd want to be here the moment that Kylie arrives."

It was unusual that Lia and Antonio would say yes to such a thing in the midst of a big family gathering so it had taken some pleading on Gabriela's part, but she was such a good kid—a sixteen-year-old who had always done well in school and brought joy to their lives. Lia hadn't felt that they could say no to letting her go out of town.

"I spoke to Kylie earlier and she was asking me about her. Wherever she is, she must not have phone service. You know how connected those two are."

Lia laughed. "Well, the two of them will be together soon enough."

The two sixteen-year-olds really did seem to have a special relationship, one that Lia and Blu had always encouraged. Over the years, they'd traded weeks of the summer with the girls— Kylie with Lia and Antonio at the villa and then Gabriela with Blu and Chase in Florence. Of course, Lia always preferred to have them with her, but she'd learned to use the time that Gabriela was away for special projects at the restaurant.

Lia reached for Gigi's hand across the table. "So have you given any more thought to your birthday? We do have to have a party, you know."

Gigi's seventieth birthday was coming up and Lia was determined to throw her a party, but as of yet, Gigi had been resistant to the idea.

"Oh, you think so?" Gigi winked. "Well, you know I would just be happy to have the whole family around me. There's not much more these old bones could want."

"Oh, stop! You're not old in the least—I mean, tell that to that husband of yours. I swear he seems more and more smitten with you as the years go by. I can only hope that Antonio will look at me that way ten years from now."

"Well, I could say that same about Antonio, you know. I don't think you need to worry about your own husband losing interest any time soon."

The two women grinned at one another and Gigi reached across the table to squeeze her friend's hand. Lia sure had been lucky in love—this was something that she was grateful for every day. How was it that nearly sixteen years had passed since the day she'd become Antonio's wife? Sixteen years of marriage and yet she still felt that same quickening in her heart and butterflies in her stomach when he looked at her a certain way, so devoted and always thoughtful about Lia knowing his heart.

Life had been good to her—in ways she never would have imagined after Arianna had passed away.

She squeezed Gigi's hand in response. "You are right about that husband of mine. He's a keeper."

Gigi looked at her phone on the table when it buzzed. "Speaking of husbands, let me take this call from Douglas and then shall we head over to Bella's?"

"Yes, perfect. I'll go pack up the dessert—I nearly forgot, and I know how much Bella is enjoying her sweets these days."

She turned to cross the kitchen as Gigi stepped outside to take her call.

FOUR

"Hi, how's it going? Were your ears burning because we were just talking about you?" Gigi grinned as she waited to hear her husband's voice on the other end of the line.

"Honey, are you with Jemma?"

"No, not yet. We're literally about to go out the door to head over there for lunch. Why? What's up?"

"Have you had the news on at all? There's been another earthquake."

"No. Where? Another one in Guatemala, you mean?"

Gigi crossed the patio to sit down, trying not to think the worst, but instant pictures of their kids—the orphans at Casa de los Niños—played through her mind like a slideshow of so many memories.

Since they'd moved to Tuscany and officially retired several years ago, it was mostly Douglas who made the trip to Guatemala on a regular basis. Gigi hadn't been back to the orphanage in a few years but she was in regular contact with Tori, who kept her informed about the children and everything that was going on there.

"Yes," Douglas said, "I did hear from Tori, so don't worry, love. Everyone at the orphanage is fine. They'd already started their rebuilding before it hit and there was no new damage there, but..."

"But what? Honey? Is Rafael okay?"

"Well, Tori says that Rafael had gone to a neighboring village—he was picking up supplies there—and she hasn't been able to get a hold of him. I'm sure he's fine, but I don't know what Jemma knows, so if you could just tell her that I'm working to get a hold of him. Tell her that there wasn't much damage at the orphanage, so almost certainly it's not so bad where he was either."

"Okay. Yes, we'll be over there shortly to keep the girls company. You'll call us when you hear anything?"

"Yes, I will and we should be on the road here in the next hour or so ourselves, so it won't be too late."

"Okay, I love you, honey."

"I love you too."

Gigi clicked off the phone and closed her eyes for a moment, saying a silent prayer of thanks that everyone at the orphanage was alright and then just as quickly saying a quick prayer for Rafael. Douglas would get a hold of him and everything would be fine. It was probably just an issue with the phone line. It was something that they'd experienced themselves while living there, so it was not beyond the realm of possibility that Rafael was simply unable to get word to them.

She breathed deeply, taking in the beauty of the vineyard that surrounded her. She never tired of spending time at Lia's and Antonio's. Everything about it was so warm and beautiful. Even though she and Douglas lived less than a half hour away, they spent many days and sometimes overnights at the villa. It was practically their home away from home, something that Lia and Antonio always stressed was exactly how they wanted their guests to feel.

With Christmas around the corner and the happy anticipation of a new baby in the family, there'd been a lot to prepare for over the past weeks. And Gigi loved every moment of it. Spending time with Lia—learning from her in the kitchen— and getting the villa ready for the holiday season was Gigi's favorite time of year.

She had to laugh when she thought about how far she'd come with her cooking abilities over the years. She'd gone from being a non-cook to someone whose Italian dishes rivaled that of any other proud Italian woman's—something that delighted her husband even though he'd swear that it had never mattered to him at all.

Gigi looked down at her buzzing phone to see that it was Jemma this time.

"Hi, sweetie. Are you two getting hungry? We should be on our way shortly."

"Okay...Gigi, have you spoken to Douglas? I texted him but I know that he and Antonio had a meeting today. I just really need to get a hold of him...did you hear about the earthquake?"

"Yes, I just got off the phone with him, actually. Honey, I'm sure that Rafael is fine. Douglas is going to keep trying to get a hold of him and he has spoken to Tori."

"Oh, he has?"

Gigi could hear the lighter tone to Jemma's voice—the tone of hope. What could she say that wouldn't crush that hope? They all needed to believe that Rafael would get a hold of them soon.

"Yes, but...but Rafael had gone to a nearby village. So Tori's not heard from him—but she did say that there wasn't damage at the orphanage...that it's unlikely to be much worse where Rafael is. Honey, I'm sure you'll hear from him soon. It's probably just the phone lines. You know how that goes sometimes there."

"I know. Okay, I just wanted to check to see if Douglas knew anything. I'd be lying if I said that I wasn't going a little batty here—you know, I'm trying not to let my mind go there but—it's hard."

"We'll be over in a few minutes. Is Bella there with you?"

"Yeah...well, not since I heard the news from Mom. She's taking a nap but I think I hear her up now. Okay. Don't worry, Gi. I'll see you soon. Thank you."

"Bye, hon. See you in a few minutes." Gigi clicked off the phone and walked toward the house just as Lia stuck her head outside the door.

"Is everything okay? Ready to go?"

"Yes, I'm ready and I'll fill you in regarding Douglas's call on the way to Bella's."

Gigi entered the kitchen and picked up the covered dishes that remained on the counter. "Is this everything?"

"Yes, the rest of it is in the car ready to go. I'm actually quite hungry now myself."

"Me too—and anxious to see the girls," said Gigi.

Gigi filled Lia in during their short drive to Isabella's.

FIVE

Isabella stretched out on top of her bed, pointing and then flexing her toes. Her hands automatically went around her stomach, which had gotten so big that she could no longer see her feet while lying down.

She hadn't gained as much weight when she'd been pregnant with Arianna, and a small part of her panicked at the thought that what had happened to Jemma could happen to her. But the doctor had assured her time and time again that there was only one healthy, growing baby boy in her womb.

She yawned and looked at the time on her phone. It was rare that she took an early nap as she had that morning, but she did so appreciate having Jemma around. Arianna was a pretty easy child as far as temperament went, but like any typical three-year-old she demanded a lot of attention. In Isabella's head, she had plenty of energy to keep up with her, but these days her body often told her otherwise, demanding short naps whenever she could manage it.

Jemma and the twins were staying with them while Rafael

was out of town. Once he returned, they'd move to one of Lia's and Antonio's guest houses, although Isabella guessed that Arianna would have something to say about that, as she loved it when the twins slept over. Isabella's parents would stay with them when they arrived, and Lucas and his family would also stay in one of the guest houses at Lia's.

Isabella loved it when everyone was altogether in Tuscany. There was nothing like it, and although preparations were sometimes a bit hectic, once everyone arrived, it was always easy and relaxed. Magically everyone pitched in and everything got done and then there were big meals, long walks, and fun outings to enjoy.

Isabella sat up in bed and picked up the picture that sat on her nightstand. It was of her and Thomas on their wedding day, Thomas looking at her with the funniest expression on his face. She, the epitome of a glowing bride, basking in his love and everything that had transpired that day. The wedding had been perfection, and Isabella could remember every detail as if it had happened only yesterday.

Thomas had planned the perfect honeymoon that had begun the day after he'd surprised her with the villa. What Isabella had thought was going to be three weeks of travel ended up being one week because they'd both been so excited to get back to their new home—to settle into their new life in Tuscany as husband and wife.

And the past four years had been good to them. She'd never seen Thomas as happy as he was while working in the vineyard. There'd been so much to learn, but with Antonio's guidance, they had a thriving business and beautiful land that rivaled any to be seen in the region.

Isabella loved her life there and couldn't imagine that she could ever be happier.

She looked toward the door as she heard giggling followed by a light knock.

"Come in."

The door opened quickly as Arianna ran across the room followed by the twins, the three of them hopping right up onto Isabella's large bed.

"Mommy? Are you finished with your rest?"

Isabella reached out to pull Arianna in close for a hug. "I think so, yes. And what are you girls up to? Did you have lunch yet?"

"Yep. Mommy fed us already," said Chloe.

"And she said to tell you that Lia and Gigi are on their way," said Daisy.

"She also said that we should ask you if we can watch a movie now. Can we, Mom? In the big room?" asked Arianna.

"Yes, I suppose that's a good idea. Why don't you three go pick one out? I'll be right in to get you set up."

"Great! Thank you, Mommy!" Arianna kissed Isabella quickly before she hopped off the bed. "Come on, girls, I know just the movie you're going to love."

Isabella smiled as the girls ran out of the room. She and Thomas had made the decision to limit Arianna's time watching television. They wanted her to grow up spending lots of time outside in the vineyard, something the little girl loved.

As a concession, though, Thomas had turned the third floor room into a big entertainment center, with comfy sofas and chairs and a big-screen TV. They'd gotten every classic and kid's movie that they both felt was appropriate, and often in the evenings and on the weekends, the three of them would spend special time upstairs watching a movie and eating popcorn. It had become one of Arianna's favorite things to do after she was good and tired from playing outside most of the day.

And lately, Isabella had not made it through a single movie without her eyes closing, something which seemed to drive her daughter slightly crazy, despite her father's explanation that Mommy was extra tired because she was growing Arianna's baby brother inside her tummy.

"Knock, knock," Jemma said from the open doorway to Isabella's room. "I hope the girls didn't wake you. I did tell Ari she had to be very quiet when she checked to see if you were awake."

Isabella laughed. "Thanks, Jem. No, I think it's time to get up. I do so appreciate the quiet time—thanks for that."

"Oh, I remember. Naps were like the biggest gift to me when I was pregnant—well, I didn't have a child to think about so I'm not sure how I'd cope a second time around. Rafael used to say that he was concerned that my normally energetic body had been invaded by aliens. I was like—yeah, your kid! Little did we know, right?"

Isabella laughed. "Yeah, I wonder if you were twice as tired with two of them as I am now with one. That idea is crazy to me."

Jemma crossed the room to sit on the bed beside Isabella, and when she did Isabella lay back and rolled to her side, patting the space beside her. "I see something on your face, girl. What's up?"

Jemma lay down next to Isabella, just as they'd done countless times over the years—two girlfriends sharing secrets and their dreams with one another from the moment they'd met and become instant friends.

"Hey, what's wrong?"

At Isabella's words, Jemma's eyes had teared up.

"Ugh. I'm trying not to freak out—honestly, but..."

"What? Tell me, Jem."

Isabella listened as Jemma filled her in on all the news that had transpired over the morning. She grabbed her friend's hand and squeezed it tight. "Oh, please don't worry, Jem—I mean, I get it. I would worry too, but I just know that Rafael is fine. He'll be phoning you any minute, and get back here to watch those gorgeous daughters of yours open up their gifts."

Jemma was nodding her head, but not looking so convinced. "I know. I'm going to try not to think about it. Well, let's go have a nice lunch with Lia and Gigi. They must be downstairs by now—I saw the car coming up the driveway a minute ago."

Isabella hoisted herself halfway up from the bed, laughing as she felt Jemma's hands on her lower back. "Thanks, pal."

"Hey, I feel your discomfort. I think it's a small miracle that you have as much energy as you have. He'll be here before you know it."

"And I can't wait. Well, assuming he doesn't decide to come right in the midst of our festivities."

Jemma nodded. "Unfortunately, I'm not sure how much you're going to be able to count on that plan."

Isabella tapped her stomach lightly. "You hear that, little guy? Would you like to come early? Today maybe?" Isabella laughed at the look on Jemma's face. "Hey, I've got some help here. It wouldn't be a bad idea."

"Not at all," said Jemma.

"I'm going to go get the girls set up with their movie. I'll meet you downstairs in a minute. And Jem?"

"Yeah?"

"Try not to worry, okay?"

"Yeah, okay. I'll try."

SIX

Blu tried to focus on the show. The Paris holiday event was one of the most important of the season and she'd worked hard to perfect everything about her collection. But now her mind was totally on her son-in-law and Jemma, who she knew would be worrying, no matter what anyone said.

She glanced at her watch, then brought up her calendar on her phone. She could make the flight out in a few hours if she canceled her dinner plans. After thinking about it for only a few seconds more, she emailed her assistant and texted Chase. Her daughter needed her, and Blu's family always came first.

Blu hadn't gotten so far in her career by being indecisive. She was used to making quick decisions and trusting her gut instinct, as it related to design or just life in general. Some things were more important than work—she'd learned that lesson well over the years. Besides, she had a stellar reputation as one of the top designers in all of Europe. Without being arrogant about it, Blu Foster could call the shots as she pleased within the industry.

She couldn't wait to get home, to be with everyone at the

villa. It had been a long exhausting week and she hated being away from her family at all, let alone an entire week.

With the holidays, Chase had been extra busy at the restaurant. So much so that he'd welcomed sixteen-year-old Kylie's request to step in alongside him in the kitchen. She'd become quite his young protégé over the years, a fact that delighted her father greatly.

Blu loved to watch the two of them cooking in the kitchen together. Kylie was like her father in so many ways, but she had Blu's style and creative flair. Unlike her older sister, Jemma, who had practically lived her teenage years in ripped jeans and t-shirts, Kylie had always loved stylish clothing and was a willing model for her mother.

Blu could hardly bear the thought that Kylie was now sixteen. Where had the time gone? She was certainly thankful that they had Jemma and the girls there. She and Chase both adored being grandparents to Chloe and Daisy, something that was a wonderful surprise to her if she was being honest with herself.

Thoughts of Jemma reminded her to check her phone messages. She'd had a missed call from Douglas. If only he had some good news, she'd feel so much better going into her last meeting of the day before she could get on her flight to Florence.

The show had been a great success and it had been followed by a few meetings with designer friends that she'd not see again well into the new year. She loved the scene and she certainly loved that they'd made the decision to move her business from San Diego to Italy all those years ago, keeping the beach house for the occasional holiday spent in California. It had been a good business move at just the right time and her career had thrived all that much more.

The years had been good to her and Chase. More in love than ever, stealing moments whenever they could—which wasn't near enough if they were tallying it all up. Yet somehow they always managed to find that quiet space together just when they most needed it. And Blu could feel that familiar yearning coming upon her now.

SEVEN

Lia met Gigi's eyes across the table. They knew each other so well after so many years that Lia knew exactly what Gigi was thinking. They still hadn't heard anything from Rafael or Douglas, and it was clear that Jemma was feeling very bothered by it all—which of course Lia didn't blame her for. She'd be worried to death if she and Antonio were in a similar circumstance.

"Honey, would you like some more pasta?" Gigi said to Isabella, her hand already scooping it up over Isabella's plate.

Isabella laughed. "Good grief. You wouldn't think that I could manage another bite—yet somehow, I'm feeling that familiar ravenous urge all over again."

Jemma smiled at her friend and lifted her own plate up so that Gigi could scoop some of the pasta for her as well. "This is really good. Is it a new sauce, Lia?"

"That one you have to ask Gigi about."

"Really?" Jemma's grin widened when she saw the funny expression on Gigi's face.

"Yes, really. It's a recipe that I got from one of my sisters. I do come from a long line of real Italian cooks, if you can believe it." Gigi was laughing. "But it's only thanks to Lia, of course, that I can actually make something that's edible."

"Oh, stop. You were never that bad," said Lia. "You just needed a little encouragement, that's all. Well, you were always a willing student, that's for sure."

Isabella put a big forkful of the pasta into her mouth. "Well, I don't care how long it's taken you, Gi, I'd say this is well worth the wait."

Gigi reached across the table for Isabella's hand. "That's exactly what Douglas says."

"The girls sure are quiet today," said Lia. "Aside from the quick kiss hello they gave us when we arrived, I've not heard a peep from them."

"They're upstairs watching Christmas cartoons," said Isabella. "I figure we'll let them have some quiet time before we bust out the hot chocolate and start decorating the tree."

Lia didn't miss the look of discomfort on Isabella's face as her hand went to her stomach. "Honey, are you feeling alright?"

Isabella sighed. "I don't know. This li'l guy has really got some kicks going today. I guess I am feeling maybe a bit more uncomfortable—but you know, it's the countdown, right?"

Gigi reached over and placed her hand on Isabella's arm. "That's right. Any day now—and don't you worry about a thing here. I think we can handle getting that tree decorated for you and minding the kids. Why don't you go get comfortable on the sofa, dear?"

Isabella smiled, and Lia's stomach twisted as it sometimes did when she caught a certain look of her granddaughter's. She looked so much like her mother, Arianna at times, that the resemblance almost took Lia's breath away. But the passing years had eased the pain of losing her daughter. Now she was just extremely grateful for the fullness of love and family that she had in her life.

"You know, I think I will take you up on that, Gi," said Isabella. "Thomas got all the boxes of decorations down from the attic, and I think everything we need is in the living room. Why don't I go get the hot chocolate going and in a few minutes, I'll call up for the girls to come down—when you all are finished eating." She stood up from the table. "And no need to rush."

"Okay, good," said Gigi.

Lia noticed Jemma glancing at her phone on the table. "No word yet, honey?"

"Nope." Jemma sighed. "Honestly, I'm really trying not to worry—not to think the worst—but why doesn't he just text me?"

"It's probably just the lines, sweetie. It always gets a little messed up there when there's any kind of a situation. Have you checked all his social media accounts?"

"Yeah, I have, and I know you're right."

She smiled but Lia could tell that it was forced.

Before Lia could speak again, Jemma's phone buzzed on the table and she was up out of her chair with it within seconds. "It's Raf! Oh, thank God!"

Lia caught Gigi's eye across the table and without speaking, she was sure that they were having the same thought.

Rafael was okay. Thank God.

EIGHT

Jemma almost couldn't believe it when she saw Rafael's name flash across her phone. It was a lifeline to her amidst the sea of doubt that she'd been weathering. Physically, she could feel herself breath again just as soon as she heard her husband's voice on the other end of the line. She turned toward the others at the table—that confirmation of his voice the final reassurance she needed—and gave a thumbs-up before she slipped outside onto the patio and burst into tears.

"Shhh. I'm okay, baby."

She could hardly get the words out. "Raf, do you have any idea how good it is to hear your voice? I've been worried sick about you."

"I know. I'm sorry. The phones weren't working and—well, it's been a little crazy around here, to say the least."

"Are you okay? Raf, you'd tell me if you weren't, wouldn't you?"

"Yes, love. I'm alright. A little shaken, but alright. How are you? How are my girls doing?"

"We're all okay, but we want you here with us. But we can

talk about that later. Tell me, what's going on? Tori said you were away when the second earthquake hit. Honey, is everyone okay there?"

Jemma knew that Rafael's heart was with her and the girls, but there was a big part of him that would always consider Guatemala and the people there his family. He felt a certain obligation—especially when it came to the children—to never forget where he had come from and what Casa de los Niños had meant to him as a child.

Rafael went quiet on the other end of the line and Jemma ached to hold him, to touch him as they spoke. "Honey, what is it?"

She heard him sigh.

"I was in one of the villages when the earthquake hit—getting some supplies that were needed at the orphanage. The village was hit pretty hard and several large buildings collapsed. Another guy and I pulled two kids—two brothers—out from a collapsed home and I've been at the hospital in the city with them for the past day. Honey, they lost their mother and grand-mother and I—I'm just trying to locate any family that I can for them."

Rafael had lost his own parents when he was very young and the orphanage had, for the most part, been the only home he'd ever known. Jemma knew that if he had knowledge of two orphaned children, he'd not be able to leave them without knowing where they were going to be cared for. And she loved him for that—even if it did seem the chances of her husband making it home in time for Christmas were growing slim.

"And? Are you having any luck?"

There was another sigh. "No, not really. The man who helped me pull them out from the collapsed building was a neighbor. He says that to his knowledge there never appeared to be any other family around. So, we're working on that."

Rafael went silent again.

"Raf? What is it?"

"Jem, it's a long shot but I was thinking that maybe I could bring the boys back with me—just for Christmas. I mean, I have to get temporary custody and of course you know all about the red tape around here, but Tori tells me that she thinks it's possible—that she knows someone here in the city that might be able to pull some strings for me."

"Do you think you can make all that happen so quickly? Honey, I would love it if you can make it home in time—I've not told the girls otherwise yet. And yes, of course you should bring them with you—if you think they're okay to travel. Honey, are they hurt?"

"No, no. I just spoke to the doctor, actually and he says they will be released in a few hours. They're shaken up, that's for sure. They know about the death of their mother and grand-mother, but I don't think it's really sunk in yet and—"

"How old are the boys?"

"Nicolas is six and Mateo is eight. They're good boys. I can tell by how they look out for one another. I—I don't think I can leave them, in any case, without being sure that they are all set to go back to Casa de los Niños. Tori has a feeling that they will end up there. They can take them there, to be sure. Oh, I don't know."

"What, Raf? What is it?"

"There's a lot of paperwork to get in order—permissions, passports—maybe bringing them back with me is a crazy idea."

Jemma smiled. She knew her husband so well. "Raf, of course it's a crazy idea and of course you're going to give it your best shot. I say, get in touch with Tori's contact and start making it happen."

Rafael laughed.

"What?" Jemma said. "You've already started the process, haven't you?"

"I spoke with him just before I called you. He says it's a long shot, but he'll do his best."

Jemma waited another few moments while Rafael went silent, imagining the look on his face before she even heard the words.

"Honey, do you have any idea how much I love you?"

She smiled. "I think I have some idea." She could hardly speak for the lump that had formed in her throat. "I love you too, Raf. When I thought something might have happened to you, I—I almost couldn't breathe. Now, just get home, okay?"

"Okay, babe. Give the girls big hugs and kisses for me, alright? I'll try to video chat at some point very soon."

"We'd like that—very soon, please. We miss your face." Jemma laughed.

"I miss your beautiful face, love. Okay, I'll keep you posted. The phones seem to be working fine now. Bye, honey."

"Bye, Raf. I love you."

"I love you too."

Jemma clicked off the phone and collapsed in one of the outside chairs near where she'd been pacing on the patio. She'd never felt so relieved to hear her husband's voice.

She smiled. Now she felt free to get into the holiday spirit with the girls around the vineyard.

NINE

Gigi assembled the tray of cookies and hot chocolate in the kitchen after insisting that Isabella go on ahead of her to put her feet up. Over the quiet sound of Christmas music, she could hear the girls laughing as they worked to unwrap each of the ornaments and place them carefully on the tree.

She smiled at the twins as they ran up to her when she entered the living room.

"Gigi, can I have one of the snowmen?" asked Chloe.

"And the blue Christmas tree is Ari's," Daisy said matter-of-factly, which caused Arianna to run over to the tray too.

"Well, actually, I made that tree for Daddy. But I'll have the reindeer, please." She turned to Chloe. "Is it okay, Chloe?"

Chloe nodded her head after it seemed that she'd thought about it for a moment. "Yes, I decorated that one for you, Ari. I hope you like it."

Gigi laughed and laid paper plates out on the small table that they had set up in the corner of the living room for the girls. "Girls, why don't you take a break from decorating to come have your hot chocolate, then?"

After the kids were situated, Gigi sat down on the sofa where Isabella and Lia were talking quietly. She reached out to take Isabella's hand. "Are you feeling better, honey?"

"Oh, I don't know. I feel a little strange, but not horrible." She rubbed her stomach. "I was just telling Lia that I wonder if this little guy is wanting to make an early appearance."

"Well, now would be as good a time as any, I suppose," said Gigi. "Is Thomas due home soon?"

Isabella looked at her phone. "Yes, and he's at a meeting nearby. He's assured me these last few weeks that he will not be more than a thirty-minute drive away. But there's no need to sound the alarms just yet. My parents just texted me saying they would be here within the hour too." She grinned at the two women sitting next to her and at Jemma, who had just entered the room. "It sure is nice to have you all here."

"Well, I think I speak for all of us, when I say how excited we are to meet this new little one," said Jemma.

"Jem, tell us what's going on with Rafael! Is everything okay?" said Isabella.

Jemma filled them in on everything, including the possibility of two more place settings for Christmas dinner.

"Well, you know what this means, don't you?" Gigi grinned at Lia.

"More shopping?" Lia laughed.

Jemma laughed too. "Well, maybe hold off until we know for sure about the boys. You know how slow things can move there. Honestly, it would be surprising if he's able to make it happen that fast, don't you think, Gigi?"

"I would say yes, but I do have an idea who the person is that Tori is speaking about. I think, given the circumstances, Rafael might be able to get the boys released to him for the holiday. It's pretty amazing what the right connections can mean there."

"Well, then we will all hope for that. It seems like it certainly would be a good thing for those poor boys. I can't imagine what they must be going through." Lia reached her hand out to Jemma. "I'm so happy and relieved that you did hear from Rafael. Of course, I was counting on the fact that everything was okay—we all were."

Gigi didn't miss the tears in Jemma's eyes. She knew the stress that the poor girl had been under the past few days, and it was a relief for them all that she'd finally gotten that phone call.

"It sure is interesting what a little perspective can do, huh?" Jemma laughed lightly. "I mean, when Rafael first talked to me about going to Guatemala, my biggest concern was whether he'd be back to open presents and celebrate Christmas with the girls. Now, with the circumstances of the boys, I'm just thankful he's okay. He may or may not make it back in time, and you know what? I think I'm okay with that."

Gigi nodded. "That's a good, good man you have there, honey. I know very few men with hearts as big as his."

Jemma nodded. "Yes, I'm a very lucky girl. That's for sure."

"As is he, my darling," Lia said as she stood up from the sofa. "Bella, I've just gotten a text from your father that he and Emily are about twenty minutes away. I'm going to leave Gigi and Jemma to finish with the girls and the decorating while I go put some lunch together for them."

Isabella hoisted herself up from the sofa. "Oh, great. I should go freshen up a bit, I suppose." She laughed. "My mom is not going to believe how big I've gotten since she last saw me."

Gigi smiled. When she'd last spoken with Emily, there'd

been no mistaking how excited she was to become a grand-mother for the second time. Emily and Richard would be staying on with Isabella and Thomas to help after the baby was born, and Gigi knew how nice that would be for Isabella.

"You go, dear. Jemma and I will finish up in the living room." Gigi looked toward Jemma, who was already stringing lights around the tree. "And when the men get home, we'll send them to work on all the outside decorations. We'll have your little paradise villa all sparkly and holiday-ready before you know it."

Isabella leaned over to kiss Gigi on the cheek. "Thank you. Really, I can't thank you both enough. You've all done so much for me lately. I owe you big time." She laughed.

"Oh, don't be silly, and don't think I've forgotten how much you helped me out when the twins were born. That's what family is for, right, Gi?" Jemma grinned.

"I couldn't say it better myself." Gigi smiled at the two girls.

Though not blood-related, Isabella and Jemma meant as much to Gigi and Douglas as if they were their own grandchil-dren, something Gigi was always extremely grateful for.

TEN

Isabella sighed as Emily's fingers worked magic on her feet. "Wow, Mom. You have no idea how good that feels."

Emily grinned. "Oh, I have some idea. I've been practicing on your father, who is more than a willing student, I might add."

Isabella pretended to put her fingers in her ears as she laughed. "That's enough. Tell me no more."

Her mother had recently started a course to get certified in massage. Isabella loved the new life that her parents had in their sleepy little village in Spain. She'd never seen them happier, and was pleased to see them taking up so many different activities during their retirement years.

"You're funny. You know your father—he's always enjoyed a good back rub."

"Where is Dad, by the way? I haven't seen him since he kissed me hello on the way in."

"Oh, I think he's got Jemma cornered out on the patio. He's taken up drawing. Did he tell you that? I think he was really anxious to show her his sketchpad."

Isabella laughed. "Dad is drawing? As in he's taking a class?"

"Oh yes, he has been for a few months now. It's just a small group of expats that get together once a week or so, but the instructor is very talented—a local guy. Your father's quite good actually, Iz. Ask him to show you later."

Isabella nodded. "Well, I think that's great. I only hope that I won't be keeping you guys from all your activities—after the baby is born, I mean. Because it sure sounds like you have a pretty busy schedule these days." She laughed lightly.

She knew that even though she had Lia and Gigi nearby, it was Emily that she would most want by her side once their little boy was born. She'd been such a godsend when Isabella had given birth the first time, and now Isabella had Arianna to look after as well.

"Oh, honey, you know there is nowhere else we'd rather be. We're planning to stay just as long as you need us, and if you change your mind after you get tired of company and send us away, we'll be right back in no time."

Isabella loved it that her parents were only a very short flight away. When they'd originally talked about moving to Europe, Isabella and the whole family had gently tried to sway them to make their home in Tuscany, but it was Spain that had captured their hearts during their travels. And no one could fault them, for the little place they had purchased was in a stunning location and every bit as lovely as Isabella's and Thomas's villa overlooking the valley.

Isabella sat up and reached out to take Emily's hand. "Well, it means a lot to me. And to Arianna. She's been asking me practically every hour when the two of you are arriving. She's going to be the happiest little girl when she gets up from her nap." Isabella looked at the time on her phone. "If she's not up within a half hour, we'll wake her. We don't need the little ones up all night." She laughed.

Jemma had taken the twins—who were not napping these days—into town for some shopping. Arianna had thrown a small fit at the unfairness of not being able to go too, having only calmed down enough to lie in her bed after Isabella had promised her that the twins could sleep over for one more night. The nap would definitely do her some good, with all the company and commotion going on.

"Oh, speaking of..." Emily grinned and winked at Isabella. "I think I hear someone coming down the stairs. Who could that be?"

Isabella stifled a laugh when she heard her daughter's giggles. "I don't know, Mom. I think that Arianna has decided that she might like to skip Christmas this year—you know, because she has so many toys already."

"Hey! Mommy!" Arianna ran into the room, heading straight for Emily, who scooped her up in her arms. "That's not true, Nana. I do really want Christmas this year."

"You do, do you?" Emily covered Arianna's face with kisses, and seconds later the girl was out of her arms and curled up next to Isabella on the sofa.

"And Mommy?"

"Yes, my love bug." Isabella reached out and tapped her daughter on the end of the nose.

"Mommy, Christmas is not only about toys, you know."

She looked so serious when she spoke that it was difficult for Isabella to answer her with a straight face.

"Oh, is it not?"

In reality, Arianna did not have too many toys. Isabella and

Thomas had tried very hard not to spoil their daughter, and she wasn't a child who asked for many things.

Arianna was shaking her head. "No, and you know that, Mommy. It's about the whole family coming together to spend time together. I get to play with the twins and the older girls. We get to eat a lot of nice food and all of the Christmas cookies we made the other day…"

"Well, pumpkin, that sounds pretty fun to me," said Emily. "And I think there might also be some presents under the tree for you."

"Oh, really?" Arianna looked at Isabella. "Mommy, can I go look?"

Isabella nodded. "Yes, go ahead. Don't shake anything and remember that there are presents under there for everyone."

"How will I know which ones are mine then?"

"Honey, do you remember what the letter A for Arianna looks like?"

"Like this? Is this right?" Arianna drew the letter A in the air with her finger.

"Excellent! You're getting so smart, Arianna," said Emily.

"Thank you, Nana." Arianna grinned at Emily before she ran off toward the tree in the far corner of the room.

Isabella laughed and then placed her hand on her stomach. "Ooh, ouch. It hurts to laugh."

"Really? Are you okay, Iz?"

Isabella stood up and leaned over to stretch her back. "Oh my. I don't know, actually." She tried to breathe through the sudden pain she was feeling in her back. "Mom, I think we might need to call Thomas."

ELEVEN

Jemma leaned back against the overstuffed chair, taking the cup of warm tea that Blu handed her. When her mother had called her from the airport earlier, Jemma had been relieved to hear about her earlier arrival. Of course, she'd tried to convince Blu that she didn't need to change her plans, but there was a relief that went along with sitting with her mother now that couldn't be denied.

It had been a crazy, emotional, busy day and Jemma suddenly felt the exhaustion that seemed to completely overwhelm her body.

"So, you hear that?" Jemma grinned.

"What's that?" Blu sat down on the sofa next to her, and Jemma knew that her mother was probably at least as tired as she was.

"Silence." Jemma laughed.

Blu laughed too. "Right, because we're the only ones who aren't smart enough to crawl into bed."

Jemma looked at the time on her phone. "You do have a point there." She leaned over to take Blu's hand. "I'm just thankful to have a quiet minute with you. Thanks for being here, Mom."

"Honey, if you don't know by now that no show or dinner or meeting is more important to me than you guys—my family—then I've done something wrong."

Jemma smiled. "I do know that. It just would have been fine for you to keep your plans—now that I know Rafael is okay, I mean. But I am very happy to see you, as we all are."

Everyone, except for Lucas and his family, had arrived that day. Jemma and the girls had moved over to Lia and Antonio's house, and before they could even think of preparing the dinner that Lia had planned, they'd gotten the call that Isabella thought she was going into labor.

Thomas had taken Isabella, along with Emily and Lia, to the local hospital and she was sent home several hours later with the knowledge that it had been false labor after all. So it had been a very late dinner, by the time everyone was home and settled again. Isabella and Thomas had opted out because Isabella could barely keep her eyes open, and Jemma had offered to keep Arianna for a sleepover with the twins.

So to have this quiet moment now with her mother, after finally putting the girls to bed, was heaven to Jemma. She glanced at her phone as she sipped her tea.

"Any word?" Blu asked.

Jemma had filled her mom in on everything that had transpired with Rafael and also the fact that she'd not heard from him since their brief conversation that morning.

"No, but I know how busy he must be. Now that I understand what he's trying to accomplish in the next few days, I'm trying to be more patient, although I can't say that the girls are having as easy of a time with it."

"Oh, well, I'm sure the moment he's able to, he'll be on the phone to them."

Blu had often remarked to Jemma how great she thought Rafael was, especially as a dad. She'd never seen him be anything less than hands-on, and she knew that Chloe and Daisy had a special relationship with their father. Jemma smiled. She was lucky, that was for sure. She had always felt Rafael's constant support for her, and she owed it to him to be just as steady for him.

While she was thinking of it, she sent him a quick text, just telling him good night and that she loved and missed him. Within seconds her phone dinged with an incoming text.

So sorry, babe. The day got away from me but things are looking very good. I love you too—so much. Big kisses and hugs to you and the girls. I will call you in the morning. xo

"There, that's better, huh?" Blu grinned at her while Jemma put the phone down beside her.

"Yes, much, actually. So, now that my mind is not so scattered, please tell me all about you. How was Paris—the Christmas show? And by the way, Kylie was looking positively gorgeous today in that new outfit you made her. I swear, she's grown up even since I saw her only a week ago."

Blu grinned and Jemma had the sense that there was a secret to be pried out of her.

"What? Mom, spill it."

"Okay, but you are absolutely the first person to know this so it can't leave this room—not until I talk to Kylie anyway."

"Go on."

"You know how she had her pictures done a few months ago? We put her portfolio together and I'd given it to a few people I know."

Jemma smiled. She remembered, alright. Kylie had bugged her incessantly about clothes and her looks, trying on outfit after outfit for Jemma and the twins, who'd been a willing audience for the younger sister that Jemma was extremely close with. At sixteen, Kyle had everything—good looks, confidence, and a personality that made Jemma very proud to call her her younger sister.

"Okay, and...?"

"And there are at least two big agencies that want to see her —one in Milan, the other in Paris. I haven't even had a chance to talk to her about it yet, but I can't even imagine how pleased she's going to be."

"She's going to flip! That's fantastic news."

"It is."

"What's wrong, Mom? You're not so sure about it, are you?"

"Well, of course I have a perspective on the whole industry. If I thought for one minute that Kylie could get caught up in body image issues or if I thought that it was going to make her grow up too fast..."

"I know, Mom, but really—I don't think you need to worry about that. Kylie is one of the strongest young women I know and I mean that sincerely, not just because she's my sister— whom I happen to adore."

"I know. You're right. And I am excited for her. She's a natural, that's for sure."

"Well, she's definitely been the model for you that I never was." Jemma smiled and stood up from her chair to give Blu a big hug.

She'd put Blu and Chase through a lot when she'd been younger, but they'd never held any of it against her. Jemma had learned a long time ago what it was to count her blessings—very much thanks to her extended family that had always surrounded her with constant love and support.

Blu stood up too and hugged Jemma to her. "I never needed for you to be anything for me, honey—but you do know that, don't you?"

"Yes, of course I do. Thanks again for being here, and I have to say that I think it is definitely time for some sleep."

"Yes, I think I should probably go check on that husband of mine. It's so wonderful to think of Chase having a full week off from the restaurant. We have to take advantage of every minute, I guess."

"Indeed you do," said Jemma. And the thought reminded her that she couldn't wait to hold her own husband that much tighter when he finally arrived home to her and the girls.

TWELVE

Blu helped Lia to carry the coffee and pastries to the patio table outside. The two of them, along with Gigi, were up before everyone else, and it felt good to have a few minutes early in the day together before it got busy real fast around the villa.

The more years that passed, the more Blu appreciated her relationship with these two women in her life. What a gift it had been to her, all those years ago, when a young Arianna had come into the hole-in-the-wall bar where she'd been working. Who knew back then that Arianna would have such a great impact on her life—that her friendship and support would come to mean everything to Blu?

She owed a lot to Arianna. They all did, but Blu knew that the only thing that Arianna had wanted—the thing that had been most important to her—was her daughter and that somehow this whole big family would continue to come together and love one another.

And they certainly had done that in a big way. Their lives were as intertwined and easy as anything Arianna could have possibly imagined. Blu was sure of that.

Gigi reached over to grab Blu's hand as she sat down next to her at the table.

"It sure is nice to have you here. Did you sleep well, honey?"

"Oh yes, Chase and I always sleep well here—almost better than in our own beds."

Years earlier, Lia had taken great care to decorate and furnish each of the guest houses that they'd added to the property over the years. There was one for each of the families and enough spare bedrooms in the main property to rival any of the biggest estates in Tuscany. It was a property to be proud of, and Lia and Antonio were always very happy to welcome anyone who came through their doors.

Lia hugged first Gigi and then Blu before she sat down at the table with them. "It makes me so happy to hear that. You know I want you both to always treat the villa as if it were your own. My life would not be complete if I didn't have the family around me at least most of the time."

"Well, it won't be long before I'm sure you'll be on babysitting duty at least a little bit," said Blu.

"Oh, that's no duty. I can't wait to get my hands on another baby." Lia grinned. "And I love having my regular play dates with Arianna. I mean, how lucky am I to be living right next to my granddaughter?"

Gigi smiled. She loved it too. "Pretty lucky, I'd say."

"Speaking of Bella, has anyone talked to her since they got home last night? I just want to know how she's feeling," said Gigi. "I think she was a little disheartened when the doctor sent her away."

"She sent me a text this morning, checking to see if Arianna was up yet. I think the girls had a pretty late night along with Jemma, so I'd love it if they all got to sleep in a bit. I told Bella not to rush over—that she should enjoy a little quiet time," said Lia.

"Well, I guess that li'l guy is just not going to come until he's good and ready." Blu laughed. "It sure would be nice, though, if it happens while we're all here. Not that we won't come back, of course, and my schedule is actually pretty light for at least a few weeks. It's Chase that will need to get back to the restaurant. But never mind—like our schedules have anything to do with the birth of Bella's baby."

"Nonsense. I know that she'd love to have everyone here to meet him, so we'll just keep hoping that it happens that way," said Lia.

"So no name yet?" asked Blu.

"Well, none that they are sharing. Bella told me that they've narrowed it down to two. I think they want to wait until he's born before deciding," said Lia.

Blu wrapped her sweater a little tighter around her. Antonio already had a big fire going in the fireplace outside, as was typical during winter mornings when they had guests, but the air that morning felt particularly chilly to her.

Lia reached out to touch her arm. "Are you cold, honey? Shall we go inside and have our coffee?"

"No, I think it feels cozy, actually. It definitely wakes one up, doesn't it?" said Blu.

Gigi nodded. "Yes, usually by the time we've had our first cup of coffee and a little bit of fresh air, I'm ready for a walk with Douglas."

"Oh yeah? That's nice. Chase and I rarely exercise at the same time these days, but we do go for walks together when we're at the beach house—which, come to think of it, has been ages ago. I'm just up way too early for him most mornings. He's always exhausted from a late night at the restaurant, so the girls and I do our best to let him sleep in.

"Well, truthfully, I know I slow Douglas down but he says it's a perfect start to his day."

"Hush. You're not slowing anyone down," said Lia.

"Who's slowing who down now?" As if on cue, Douglas walked up behind Gigi, kissing her on the neck.

Gigi laughed. "Oh, you're too kind to me."

"I'm not kind." Douglas laughed. "I just happen to love spending time with my gorgeous wife."

"Sit." Gigi pushed the chair out next to her.

"Are you all warm enough out here?" Douglas walked over to the fireplace and added another log before he came back to take the seat next to Gigi.

"Yes, thank you very much." Lia handed Douglas the cup of coffee that she'd poured for him. "Here, Douglas, help yourself to a pastry—fresh from the bakery this morning and still warm out of the oven."

"Oh, you don't have to twist my arm. They look delicious." He reached for one and took a big bite. "So what's the plan for today, ladies? I've heard rumors about some things that need to be done outside."

"I think Thomas could probably use some help at their place. Bella had some lights and decorations that she wanted put up outside," said Lia. "I think pretty much everything here is covered."

"Unless you want to help us with some cooking today." Gigi winked.

"I would help you with some cooking, my love." Douglas laughed. "The question is, would anyone want to eat my cooking?"

Lia laughed. "Why don't you leave the cooking to us? And Chase has requested the kitchen during the afternoon hours. I can't wait to see what he's got going for his menu, actually. I know that Antonio had mentioned something special that he wanted to do for the kids—it may or may not involve a Santa suit, so it's possible he could use some help in that department."

Douglas put both hands on his stomach. "Well, that is concerning, isn't it? Who do you suppose is going to get the honor of that role, besides the guy with the biggest stomach these days?"

Gigi laughed, placing her own hand on top of Douglas's. "Your stomach is just fine, honey." She turned to the rest of the women at the table. "This man is more fit than the day I married him, and every day he just gets better and better."

Douglas leaned over to kiss Gigi on the lips. "Oh, so now who's being too kind?" He stood up with his coffee in hand. "I see Antonio out in the vineyard. I'll leave you ladies to it while I go chat with him about the day."

"See you later, honey." Gigi turned her attention to Lia. "So who are we still expecting? Just Lucas and his family, is that right?"

"Yes, I think they get in around two today," said Lia. She turned toward Blu. "And Rafael? Still no news?"

"No, he's still working on it and still hopeful that they can be on a flight tomorrow."

Blu felt a lot better knowing that Jemma and Rafael were on the same page. If he didn't make it home in time, it would be because of the tugging of his heart toward two little boys who were suddenly having a very different Christmas than what they'd been expecting.

Jemma had shared with Blu that she and the girls would be

fine. Yes, it would be sad if their father couldn't be with them at Christmas, but it was also an opportunity to share something important and special with the twins. That's what Jemma was focusing on now.

"Well, whatever happens, we'll make sure that Jemma and the girls have a wonderful Christmas," said Lia.

Blu smiled. "Yes, whatever happens, it will be another memorable holiday together—that we can always count on around here."

THIRTEEN

The next few days went by quickly for Lia. With the arrival of Lucas, Kate, and Annie, the villa was now full and she couldn't be happier. Gabriela had finally arrived home the day before, after being stuck in a snowstorm during the skiing holiday with her friend. She and Kylie had shut themselves up in Gabriela's bedroom, and Lia had hardly seen her daughter since. She didn't really mind, though. They were good kids, and Lia knew that Kylie couldn't wait to share all her modeling news with Gabriela, who would be just as pleased for her good friend.

Only Rafael was still not there, and they were all holding out hope that somehow he and the boys would get the papers needed to board a flight that would have them arriving the next day—Christmas Day. In the meantime, there were lots of meal preparations to be done and Lia was happy for all the help.

Lia turned toward Gigi, who was helping her choose vegetables at the market. "Do you think that's everything? We've got the salad covered and enough sweet potatoes to feed a small army. Chase is picking up our meat order at the butcher's this morning and I figured we'd pop around to the bakery after lunch—just to have a look." Lia winked.

"And what time are we meeting the girls?"

They'd made a plan to have lunch at Thyme because they hadn't managed to carve out a meal there until now. Gabriela and Kylie were watching the younger girls so that Jemma and Isabella could get away for a little while. Blu was out running an errand and promised to meet them there as well.

Lia turned her attention back to Gigi. "Oh, sorry. Yes, I told the girls we'd be there by two o'clock—and that they should come hungry. There's a few new dishes on the menu that I'd like you all to try."

"Well, you certainly don't have to twist my arm."

Lia laughed. It was a regular weekly occurrence for her and Gigi to share a meal at her restaurant. It was always the best part of Lia's week and something that they hadn't done recently, due to all the holiday planning and company in and out of the villa.

Lia looked over the items in her basket one more time, before heading to the checkout. She could hardly remember a time when she didn't have the local markets and wonderful fresh ingredients at her disposal. She always felt such a sense of home when she shopped and meandered around the small village where she'd grown up—where she and Antonio had first fallen in love.

Gigi looked at her and grinned. "Am I to assume that was a happy sigh?"

"Oh, if I sighed it was happy alright." Lia leaned over to hug her friend as the cashier rung up her order. "You know, I just love this time of year so much. I love having you all here, the cooking, the decorations, the kids—well, I don't think I'm telling you anything you don't already know."

"I know what you mean. It does feel very special. And I always think that one year can't top the last but then somehow magically it does. I think we're just really blessed, aren't we, my friend?"

"Who would have thought..."

Lia saw the question on her friend's face as they finished putting the groceries in the trunk of the car.

"I just never would have thought—all those years ago, just after Arianna had died—that I'd be able to forgive myself, let alone end up feeling so happy and fulfilled. I mean, if you could have heard the thoughts in my head back then...I was beating myself up pretty hard for all the time I'd lost with Arianna and then everything with Antonio—"

"Everything with Antonio was exactly as it should have been," Gigi interrupted her. "That man could have done nothing but love you, forgive you. It's plain as day that the two of you belong together."

"Oh, I know. Don't get me wrong, and if Antonio knew I was even speaking about this, it would drive him slightly insane." Lia laughed quietly. "Antonio's love healed me, Gigi. It really did."

Gigi looked thoughtful as they both got into the front seat of the car. When Lia placed the keys in the ignition, Gigi reached out to stop her from starting the car.

"You know what I think?"

"What?"

"I think your love healed Antonio also, and I also don't think you were as broken as you think you were—that you would have gone on and made a success of the restaurant and your life here in Tuscany regardless of having Antonio back in your life again."

"Really? Why do you think that? I felt so lost back then—when I first moved here."

"Because you've been so strong your whole life. Only a strong person—a strong mother—could do what you did for your daughter when you were too young to care for her properly. And then you came to her—right when she needed you most. Even without knowing the depths of what that meant at the time, I know how much that meant to Arianna. To her, it was the most incredible gift that she'd ever received."

Lia couldn't help her eyes filling with tears as she listened to her friend. She hardly ever cried about Arianna any more, but the holidays always made her feel just slightly melancholy with memories and all the time that she'd never had with her daughter.

She swiped her hand across her eyes and looked over at her friend sitting next to her. "Thank you, Gigi. I have no idea how I got so lucky to have you in my life, but you always seem to know the exact words I need to hear." She leaned over to hug her. "I really love you."

Lia didn't miss Gigi swiping at her own eyes. "I love you too, honey. Good grief, it must be the holidays, or we're just getting sappier and sappier in our old age."

Lia laughed as she started the car. "Well then, let's go meet our girlfriends and have a little fun, shall we?"

Gigi nodded. "Let the holiday festivities begin, I say!"

FOURTEEN

Isabella looked around at the women that she'd grown so close to over the years. No matter what else was going on, whenever possible, they tried to share at least one meal at Thyme together. It had become a tradition and a tribute to Arianna, the one person responsible for weaving the tapestry of family and friendships that now sat around the table with one another.

Isabella stared at the photo on the wall. It was the most perfect picture of her birth mother with Lia. Lia had told Isabella the stories of their travels together in Tuscany so many times that Isabella felt almost as if she'd been there with them herself.

She felt a small pang of something sad. It wasn't often that she felt deep sadness about Arianna—time had healed a lot of those wounds. But lately, with the pregnancy and her hormones all out of whack, she could feel the unshed tears every once in awhile. Of course she had Emily and her grandmother, but how she would have loved for Arianna to know her children.

She pushed the thought back and tried to focus on the conversation happening around her.

"Sorry, what was that, Lia?"

Lia was asking her something on behalf of the chef, who stood waiting in the doorway.

"Oh, I was just wondering if you want to try the new veal dish. We've got the usual pastas coming, but I'm not sure how hungry you and Little Man are feeling."

"Well, you know Little Man. He's always up for food." Isabella laughed and rubbed her stomach. "Whatever am I going to do when I don't have pregnancy as an excuse for my appetite? And actually, I think I'll pass on the meat, Lia. I'm feeling a little odd—well, every other minute these days, right?"

"Okay, honey, suit yourself. Do you want me to get you something else? Some soup maybe?"

"Soup would be perfect, thanks."

Jemma leaned over to whisper in her ear. "Are you doing okay? For real? Because you know we'd all understand if you're not up for this right now."

"Oh no. It feels good to get out of the house. I've been spending a lot of time in bed the last few days—well, thanks to you all helping to keep my child occupied."

"Oh, please. Arianna is a little joy and the twins really do most the work, don't they?" Jemma laughed. "They all keep each other occupied. And really, Kylie and Gabriela couldn't be sweeter. And Annie? Wow, she's gotten so big since I last saw her. I think she must be around eleven or twelve now? Is that right?"

"Twelve. Oh, I feel bad. I've hardly even had a chance to visit with them since they arrived. I really hope Lucas can stay on a few days longer. Kate told me that they were going to see what they could do about changing their plans. I promised

them I'd have more energy once this child was out of me."
Isabella laughed.

"Girl, how quickly you forget about the sleepless nights."

"Oh, let's only think good thoughts about sleep, please."
Isabella grinned.

Blu laughed from across the table as she passed a heaping dish of pasta to Jemma. "Well, I can't speak for everyone, but I'm pretty sure that you'll be able to get some help during the day—to steal a little quiet time as needed."

Isabella laughed as both Lia's and Gigi's hands shot up in the air.

"Yep, we are more than happy to be on baby duty," said Lia.

"And of course you have Emily staying with you, so we might have to wait in line, I suppose," said Gigi.

"Thank you all. You have no idea what it means to me to have so much support. I can't even imagine not being near you—during a time like this or any time, really."

"And I can't imagine not having you near us, honey," said Lia. "And on that note, if everyone has everything you need, I'd like to propose a toast." Lia lifted her glass of wine up in front of her and waited for everyone else to do the same. "To old friends, dear family, and the new life to be upon us. And to Arianna, for having the foresight to see the difference that she was making in each of our lives so long ago. Happy holidays and I love you all."

"Cheers." They all responded with the clinking of glasses and words of love and appreciation.

"Thank you, Lia." Isabella took a sip of her sparkling juice and tried to focus on the conversation that was going on around her.

"Sorry. Excuse me. I'll be right back." It was at least the

third time that Isabella had had to get up to use the ladies' room since she'd been there, and she was trying not to be embarrassed by it.

She slid her chair back, and as soon as she stood up to walk she nearly slipped right after she felt the swoosh of something wet.

"Bella!" Jemma was up from the table in an instant to grab Isabella's arm.

"Oh wow! Ladies, I think I'm going to have to bow out of dessert."

FIFTEEN

Gigi stifled a yawn and felt Douglas's arm go around her tighter. It had been a long night and even though she'd tried to get some sleep, she knew exactly where she'd be first thing in the morning.

They were all there in the waiting room. When Isabella had arrived at the hospital the night before, she'd been admitted right away, but Thomas's updates throughout the night were to tell them that they should all get some sleep. The baby probably wasn't coming before morning.

Gigi watched the girls playing in one corner of the room. They'd all been allowed to open one present that morning, which meant new toys to occupy them during the wait. It had been a bit of a debate as to whether they should make the thirty-minute drive or wait at home, but in the end, Thomas had told them that he and Isabella didn't mind at all if they wanted to be there at the hospital.

Gigi stood up to stretch and caught Kylie's eye from across the room where she was sitting with Gabriela. She crossed the room to sit down beside her.

"So, how excited are you, little Miss Model-to-Be?"

Kylie grinned. "I know, can you believe it? Beyond excited! Well, I still have to meet with the agencies but Mom says that she'd bet money on me signing with one of them."

Gabriela grinned next to her. "I'm so excited for you, but I hope it doesn't mean that I won't see you as much. Because that, I'm not ready for."

Kylie placed her arm around her friend's shoulder. "Nah, I'll always have time for my bestie. Besides, you've been pretty busy yourself."

"This is true. But let's not talk about any of that right now. We still have many days together."

Gigi smiled. "You two sure are good girls, you know that?"

Kylie and Gabriela grinned at one another.

"We've had good role models, I guess." Kylie winked and Gabriela got up to give Gigi a hug.

"We love you, Gigi."

"I love you too, sweetie." Gigi stood up again. "Well, I'll leave you two to your girl talk."

Jemma came over to hand her a cup of coffee. "I figured you might be able to use this."

"Thanks, honey. So what's the latest from Rafael? Did you tell him that our Christmas meal has been postponed until further notice?"

"Oh yeah." Jemma looked at her phone. "Well, for all I know, he might be on the plane right now. The last I heard, he was waiting at the airport for a courier who was supposed to be bringing the passports for the boys."

"Well, that would be good news."

"Yeah, then I think his phone died or something because we got cut off mid-sentence. I've decided not to stress about anything. He'll get here when he gets here. I think the girls are all having a nice little adventure here at the hospital in the meantime." Jemma laughed.

"Right. And any minute, I expect we'll get some baby news."

"Thomas hasn't been out for awhile now, so I'm thinking that might mean they are having this baby as we speak. Oh, I can't wait to meet him."

"Me too. Thanks again for the coffee."

Gigi walked around the room. She couldn't seem to make herself sit still for long, and the hospital had been quiet enough that morning that they'd been able to give them an entire waiting area for the family.

"You should have worn your sneakers, darling."

Gigi jumped at the sound of Douglas's voice in her ear. "My feet are fine." She laughed. "I just want to know what's going on in there. I hope everything's alright."

Douglas reached for her hand. "I'm sure it's fine. You know how these things go. It was a long time when she delivered Arianna too."

"You're right. How about you, honey? I noticed that you didn't seem to be sleeping very well yourself last night. Is everything okay?"

"Oh, yes. I suppose it's just all the excitement. I guess it affects me too—even though I don't do half the work that you and Lia do to get ready for everyone. You two have really outdone yourself this year."

Gigi laughed. "You say that every year."

"And every year just gets better and better—like you, my love." He turned her so that he could kiss her fully on the lips, causing the girls playing in the corner to erupt with giggles.

"We have an audience, my dear." Gigi winked at him. It shocked her sometimes, that after all these years of marriage—eighteen years, to be exact—Douglas still caused her stomach to flutter when he flirted with her. After all these years, he had only grown more affectionate, something that Gigi never would have thought possible. She'd been lucky in love; that was something she never took for granted.

"So, no news yet?" Lia walked up to her smiling. She and Antonio had just arrived after taking care of a few things back at the villa.

"Not yet. But in this case, I think that no news is good news."

They sat down and Gigi smiled as she watched Blu with Chase across the room. They were sitting on one of the small sofas, hand in hand, talking quietly to one another. Gigi thought the couple had never looked happier, despite their busy schedules and struggle to find time together, something that Blu had shared with Gigi and Lia not long ago. She knew that the time at the villa was good for their relationship. It was good for them all.

"Gigi, penny for your thoughts." Arianna had come over to where Gigi sat and was grinning up at her.

Gigi laughed. "Do you think so?"

Arianna nodded and held out the book that was in her hand. "Will you read this to me, please? Nana gave it to me for Christmas. It's all about being a good big sister."

Gigi took the book from her hand and lifted the little girl up onto her lap. "Sure I will. What a great idea. And I think you're going to be the best big sister anyone ever had."

Arianna's eye grew wide. "You do?"

"Sure I do. Are you getting excited to meet your baby brother soon?"

"Uh-huh. When he is coming, Gigi? I want to see Mommy and Daddy."

Arianna's lip trembled slightly and before Gigi could say another word, Emily appeared through the waiting room doors.

"Nana!" Arianna jumped off Gigi's lap and ran straight to Emily.

Emily scooped her up, grinning from ear to ear. "Arianna—everyone—the newest addition to the Jordan family is here!"

SIXTEEN

Isabella felt the tears running down her face as they placed her son on her chest.

Emily kissed her quickly on the cheek. "He's beautiful, honey. I'll go tell the others—leave you two alone for a little while."

"Okay, thanks, Mom."

"Oh, honey."

She felt Thomas's kiss on her sweaty forehead.

"You did so good, baby."

She turned her head slightly to look at him. "Isn't he beautiful?"

Thomas's fingers gently touched the back of their son's head. "I can't believe all the hair—much more than Arianna had."

Isabella leaned down to kiss her baby. She'd seen all the dark hair too before the nurse had placed the little blue cap on his head.

"I still can't believe he's really here."

Thomas seemed to be at a loss for words and when Isabella

looked at him, she could tell he was as choked up with emotion as she was.

It was funny how, in one instant—the moment they'd placed her son on her chest and she looked down at his sweet face—her heart had immediately expanded with love. It was the same love she'd been experiencing all throughout her pregnancy but magnified a thousand times. And more importantly, she now understood what other mothers said about having a second child. And in that instant her fears about not loving him enough had vanished.

Isabella laughed as she looked at him and his eyes widened. "I think it's time to name you, little one." She looked over at Thomas. "What do you think? Are you feeling either of the names?"

They'd narrowed their choices down to Antonio and Richard—they would have a child named after one of the strong men in their lives, that much they'd decided on.

Thomas looked intently at their son. "You know, I'm not so sure that I am. Is that bad?"

Isabella laughed quietly. "No, I'm not so sure now either. What do you think about Thomas? Do you want him named after you, honey?"

Thomas grinned. "No, he's definitely not a Thomas. Do we have to decide right now?"

Isabella thought about it for a second. "No, I don't think so, but I want our son to have a name soon." She laughed. "Are you thinking he will reveal it to us?"

"I am, actually, yes. Let's get to know him a little bit—a few hours, I mean, not days or anything."

Isabella leaned over to kiss her husband. "I can live with

that." She grinned. "What do you think about bringing Arianna in to meet her baby brother?"

"Are you ready to meet your big sister, little guy?" Thomas whispered to their son as Isabella rubbed her hand across his bare back under the blanket that covered them both.

She couldn't stop looking at the bundle of perfection that now nestled up against her chest. She pushed aside a little of the blanket to create even more contact with her baby's skin. She loved the feel of him against her. It was as if her body knew that she wasn't quite ready to give up that closeness that she'd had with him inside her for the past months.

He let out the tiniest of cries and then immediately stared at her with wide eyes. How did she look to him, his vision still adjusting to so much activity outside her womb?

"Hello, precious boy. I'm your mommy." She leaned down to kiss him on the nose, laughing as his eyes shut, then popped back open as he let out a quiet noise. "We sure are happy to meet you. In fact, you have a whole big family out there waiting to meet you. You're going to be so loved, little one."

As if on cue, the door opened and Thomas walked in with Arianna, who had one hand in his and the other holding a stuffed bear.

As soon as she saw Isabella, she let go of her father's hand to rush over to the bed, holding the blue bear out in front of her. "Nana helped me pick this out—it's for my brother. Oh, can I see him please?"

Isabella laughed as she wrapped the blanket around the baby so that she could turn him around to meet his sister. "Of course you can, sweetie. I think he's very excited to meet you. Come over here—right by Mommy."

Arianna stepped next to the bed and reached her finger out

to touch her brother on the face. "Mommy, I know to be very gentle with him. Daddy already told me that, right, Daddy?"

Thomas laughed from behind her. "That's right, honey. You're doing a great job. Go ahead, introduce yourself to your baby brother."

"Hi, Sammy, I'm Arianna." She patted him gently on his arm. "I'm your big sister."

Isabella and Thomas looked at one another and both laughed at the same time.

"Honey, why did you call him Sammy?"

Arianna shrugged her shoulders. "That was the name of the baby brother in my book. Sammy kind of looks like him." She looked over at Thomas. "Don't you think so, Daddy?"

Thomas was grinning as he came closer to reach for Isabella's hand. "What do you think, honey?"

"Samuel—Samuel Richard Jordan." Isabella squeezed Thomas's hand. "I love it, honey."

"Well, then Sammy it is." Thomas scooped Arianna up to cover her face with kisses while she squealed to be let down. "You've just named your baby brother, young lady."

Arianna, hands on hips after Thomas had set her back down, looked up at her father. "Daddy, everyone needs a name, of course."

Isabella grinned. "Well, that is certainly true."

The nurse had come in to take the baby for a few minutes, leaning down with him first so that Arianna could give him a gentle kiss on the cheek.

Isabella's eyes misted with tears for about the hundredth time in the last few hours. "Now, let's have Daddy lift you up here so that I can have a little cuddle with my big girl."

Isabella hugged her daughter close as Arianna chatted about

the twins, the waiting room, and her new baby brother. The weariness that suddenly overtook her did not compete with the love she had for her family, and as she smiled over at her husband, Isabella knew that the memories they'd already created together that morning would be some of the best of her life.

SEVENTEEN

Jemma laughed as Chloe and Daisy came flying down the hill on their toboggan.

"Wow! That was pretty fast, huh?" said Blu, adjusting the girl's stocking caps.

Jemma finished zipping up Arianna's coat. "There you go now. All bundled up. Are you ready to have a turn?"

"Yes, but not by myself."

"I think you can all fit on the sled if you hold on to one another real tight, okay? And put Ari in the middle."

"Okay, Mom." Chloe reached for Arianna's hand. "Come on, let's go."

"This was a great idea for this morning," said Blu. "I didn't even know this place existed."

"I didn't either. A friend of mine told me about it when I mentioned that it was rough having some snow, but not enough to really do anything with it. I thought the kids were going a little stir-crazy inside—and I think it's good to try to take Arianna's mind off missing her parents. She's been really good but she was a little emotional this morning."

"I heard Lia say that Thomas was going to take her to the hospital with him after lunch. And they'll be home soon. I think Isabella should be released tomorrow..."

"Yes, that's the plan. Then we'll get lots of baby time." Jemma grinned thinking about the conversation she'd had with Rafael earlier that morning. He'd teased her that being around baby Sam was going to make her want another. She'd teased him right back that that was never going to happen if her husband continued to be halfway around the world away from her.

"What's that look?"

"Oh, I was just thinking about Rafael."

"I must say that you're being very patient, honey."

"Well, there's not much I can do about it. I think he'll be here any day. And it sounds like the boys will be able to come for at least a few weeks. But I don't even want to think about him leaving again right now. I'm so lucky to have you all. You've been such a big help with the girls. And of course with Christmas and all the company, Chloe and Daisy have been pretty preoccupied."

"And what about the boys? Jem, do you think maybe Rafael isn't going to want the boys to go to the orphanage?"

Jemma felt a shiver of apprehension. She had, in fact, had the thought that Rafael was growing more and more attached to the boys—and how could she fault him for that? But adding two more children to their family—just like that? She really couldn't imagine it.

"Oh, man—well, don't think I've not had the thought. He certainly hasn't said anything like that, but—"

"But knowing Rafael..."

"Exactly." Jemma grinned. "And I love him for his heart, of

course. Let's not get my head going there just yet." She laughed. "I just want to focus on them getting here before it's time for all of us to leave again."

"It's gone fast, hasn't it? I'm trying to move a couple of meetings so that I can stay a few more days, but then again, I guess that depends on when you're going back."

"What about Chase?"

"Yeah, he's going to have to head back the day after tomorrow, regardless. His main chef is going on vacation next week."

"Oh, that's too bad. It does seem like you two have had some nice time together." Jemma winked. She hadn't missed the fact that Blu and Chase had had several late mornings in their guest house, and she couldn't be happier for them. They were both so busy, and Jemma knew from her own experience how important it was to a relationship to have that time to connect.

"Whatever are you talking about?"

"Mom, you're blushing!" Jemma laughed.

"Oh, stop. I am not!"

"Okay."

"No, it has been nice—really nice, actually. Personally, I think we need to start slowing down a bit. Chase is open to it. Maybe that's what the new year has in store for us; who knows?"

"Well, I'm all for that. I think you both work too hard."

"Ready, Mommy?" Chloe was screaming from the top of the small hill.

"Yes, come on, lovies. Hold on tight!" Jemma shouted back just as they started charging down the hill screaming at the top of their lungs.

"That was so much fun!" Arianna yelled as she got up from the sled. "Let's do it again!"

"Yes! Can we, Mom?" said Daisy.

Jemma looked at the time on her phone. "Okay, we have time for one more, then I thought I'd take you girls out for some hot chocolate.

"Yes! I'm so down with that, Mom," said Chloe as she gave her a thumbs-up and raced up the hill after her sister and Arianna.

Jemma and Blu looked at one another and laughed.

"I'm so down with that? Where does she come up with these things?" said Blu.

"Well, that's a new one. I'm as stumped as you are." Jemma laughed. She watched her daughters make their way up the hill, both of them hand-in-hand with Arianna. "I don't know what I'd do without those girls. They sure do keep things interesting, don't they?"

"You can say that again. How do you think Arianna is going to do once they are home with Samuel?"

"Well, so far she seems to have nothing but love for him." Jemma laughed. "Having to share with her parents once they are home could be another story, I guess. That's one thing that you don't really have to worry about with twins. I rarely get the sense that Chloe and Daisy have any jealousy toward one another, do you?"

"Not at all. I think they're best friends—two little peas in a pod."

"I sure hope they stay that way—always one another's biggest supporter. That's how I want them to be. I can't think of anything better than having a sister." Jemma didn't even think about the words until they were out of her mouth. She looked at Blu and laughed lightly. "I didn't mean anything by that."

Over the years, it was almost as if the true facts of her upbringing had been forgotten. Blu would always be the mother that raised her. It had been shocking to find out the truth so many years ago—that Blu was really her older sister. Jemma didn't think things could ever be the same again when she'd first found out.

But somehow it had all felt right. Once the dust had settled and a lot of time had passed, Linda had only ever been her grandmother and Blu was still Mom.

Blu grinned at her and hugged her close. "I know you didn't. And you're a great mother, Jemma. I don't know if I tell you that enough. I really admire the woman you've turned out to be."

Jemma's eyes instantly teared up. "Awww, thanks. That means a lot to me. It's funny, out of everything I've done, I would say that I'm most proud of those two rugrats." She laughed as she spoke and the kids came barreling down the hill for their final run.

Arianna jumped out of the snow where she'd landed, all smiles and laughing with the twins. "Aunt Jemma, thank you so much. This was the best morning ever!" She walked over to hug Jemma around the legs.

"You're welcome, sweetie. I'm glad you girls had fun. Now who's ready for some hot chocolate?"

"Me!"

All three of the girls raised their hands.

"Mom, will you please tie my hat? It came loose," said Daisy.

"Sure, honey." As Jemma bent down to tie her daughter's hat tighter under her chin, Daisy quickly kissed her on the nose.

"I love you. You're the best Mommy ever!"

Jemma quickly swiped her tears away. "I love you too, pumpkin."

EIGHTEEN

The house was so quiet. Isabella debated getting up to check on Arianna, but when she'd done so five minutes before, her daughter had been happily coloring at the small table in her bedroom. *She's fine. Enjoy the peace, Isabella.*

Thomas had left for a meeting and her parents had gone off somewhere with Lia and Antonio. Gigi was coming over in a few minutes to get Arianna so that she could go play with the twins, but for now, it was only Isabella and Sam—her beautiful baby boy.

She smiled down at her sleeping son as she rocked him. Thomas had gotten her the rocking chair when she'd been pregnant with Arianna. It sat near the living room window, and from it Isabella had her favorite view of their land.

Samuel stirred, a small smile coming to his lips, which made Isabella smile too. She's been home now for two nights and imagined her new normal routine was still sorting itself out. Thankfully, with Emily and Richard there, she'd been able to catch little naps during the day while they looked after the baby and Arianna when she wasn't over at Lia's with the twins.

Isabella loved that everyone had been there to welcome her son into their family. It had been a special Christmas season, one that wasn't over yet. She couldn't wait for the official Christmas dinner at Lia's and Antonio's that was happening that night—it would be the first time out for her with the baby and she was looking forward to it.

She said a little prayer in her head that Rafael was making his way home. Jemma had been so very patient, but Isabella knew her friend well. Jemma was missing her husband and the girls needed to see their father. But they would work everything out, including what would happen with the boys.

Isabella looked toward the front door when she heard a light knock. She could see Lucas looking at her through the window and motioned for him to come in.

"Hi, come on in," Isabella smiled at Lucas as he walked in the door. She hadn't really been able to spend that much time with him, Kate, and Annie since their arrival, and she welcomed the chance for her birth father to meet his grandson properly.

"I hope I'm not bothering you. Gigi hinted that now might be a good time for me to come see my beautiful daughter and grandkids. She's on her way over shortly." He grinned at her as he walked across the floor and bent to give her a kiss on the cheek. "Oh, he looks so peaceful."

Isabella laughed. "He wasn't quite so peaceful a half hour ago—and yes, now is the perfect time to have a little visit. It's been so busy that I've hardly had the chance to say hello. Please sit." She motioned to the sofa opposite her. "So how are you all doing over at Lia's? Is everything comfortable and okay?"

"Oh, please. Everything is perfection, as normal." Lucas laughed. "I don't know how Lia does it, but that little guest house she has us in—it's our home away from home. Kate and

Annie love how cozy it is, and you know how much I enjoy staying at the vineyard."

"Good. I'm glad. And she loves having you."

"So, how are you doing, Bella? Are you getting any sleep?"

"I am—thanks to my parents and everyone's help, really. I don't know how people possibly do it—without any support like that."

Lucas nodded. "I vaguely recall, although it's been awhile for us. Kate says to tell you hi. She and Annie have gone to do a bit of shopping, but she really wants to carve out some time with you before we leave—as does Annie, I might add."

"I would love that." Samuel stirred slightly in her lap. "Let me go get Arianna. She'll be excited that you're here. Do you want to hold your grandson?" Isabella grinned at Lucas.

"Absolutely."

Isabella adjusted Samuel's blanket a little tighter around him before getting up to place him in Lucas's arms. His eyes immediately popped open and a very sleepy-looking yawn followed.

Isabella laughed and sat down on the sofa next to them. "Sammy, say hello to your grandpa." She and Lucas both laughed at the perfect little smile on his face. "That's gas for sure —but how sweet is he?"

Lucas looked down at Samuel, and Isabella didn't miss the tears in his eyes. "Hello, grandson. It's very nice to meet you."

Isabella reached over to pull the baby blanket back just a bit. "You know, I think he has your nose."

"Oh yeah?"

"Yep, I see a very strong resemblance—of which he'll be proud of, I'm sure."

Lucas reached out to take Isabella's hand, giving it a

squeeze. "Bella, I'm so proud of you. You've just turned out to be this incredible wife and mother. I can see how happy you and Thomas are and—well, I just want you to know that nothing could make me happier."

Isabella leaned over to give him a quick kiss on the cheek. "Thank you. That really means a lot to me."

She felt the emotion welling up inside her. The connection that she felt with her birth father—with Lucas—had been a surprising one to her—and to both of them really. They'd been cheated out of many years together, but neither of them had let that fact keep them from having an honest and real relationship. And their bond had only grown stronger over the years.

Isabella was incredibly grateful for the support and love of her parents. Somehow they'd managed to fold Lucas and his family right into their lives as if they'd been there all along.

"Grandpa!"

Isabella laughed as Arianna came charging toward where they sat on the sofa. "Careful, Ari, Grandpa's holding Sammy."

Arianna squeezed in between them, kissing first Samuel on the cheek and then her grandfather. "Grandpa, watch his head. He's very fragile."

"Okay, honey. Thank you for telling me. Ari, what do you think of your baby brother?"

Arianna grinned. "I think he's pretty cool."

Lucas laughed. "Well, that's good. I bet he thinks you're pretty cool as well. And by the way, have I told you lately how big you're getting?"

"Grandpa, I'm already three, you know. How old is Annie?"

"Annie is twelve—and by the way, she can't wait to see you today."

Arianna turned toward Isabella. "Mommy, can I go over to play with Annie?"

"Sweetie, Gigi is coming over to get you in a few minutes. I think Lia has a special cookie-decorating request for you girls this afternoon."

"Goodie! I love decorating cookies!"

"I know you do, sweet girl. I have an idea. While I give your brother a diaper change, why don't you see if Grandpa wants to read you a story—one of your new books, maybe?"

Arianna looked at Lucas. "Grandpa? Is that a good idea?"

Lucas laughed and touched Arianna on the tip of the nose. "I think that's a perfect idea."

NINETEEN

Gigi squeezed Douglas's hand as they started out toward Isabella's.

When they didn't have their arms full, they would walk the easy ten minutes to the neighboring villa. When Gigi had first learned about Thomas's surprise to his wife on their wedding day, she couldn't have imagined anything more perfect. Both Isabella and Lia had been absolutely delighted that they would be neighbors.

She turned her attention toward Douglas. "Thanks for walking with me, honey."

"It's my pleasure. And what do you and the lovely Arianna have planned for today?"

Gigi's breath caught the way it sometimes did at the mention of Arianna's name out loud. How easily her mind could flash back to all those years ago when she'd cared for another little girl, so like the granddaughter that she'd never know. How was it possible that so many years had passed?

She smiled. "Well, I'm going to bring her back to the house. Kate is due back soon with Annie, and Lia has the idea to do a big cookie-decorating with the girls this afternoon. Kylie and Gabby are going to help, so we can give the moms a break."

"That sounds lovely. I'm sure that Bella is really appreciating the help."

"Well, she has plenty of willing babysitters here right now. Not that she won't once everyone leaves—I know that Lia is always willing to watch Arianna or the baby, and of course, I'll be volunteering to come up as needed." Gigi stopped for a moment, giving Douglas a quick kiss. "Honey, I still pinch myself some days—about the fact that we're living here. It was a good decision, wasn't it?"

Douglas grinned. "It was, my love. Any decision that makes you happy every day is a good decision in my book."

He was teasing her and she grinned. "Oh, is that so? And that should be pretty easy then, because as long as I'm with you, I'm pretty darn happy."

Douglas grabbed her around the waist and did a little dance move with her right there in the middle of Bella's driveway, dipping her and then kissing her full on the lips as he brought her up and close to his chest."

"Oh, heavens. You've got some moves there, mister." She laughed.

"You still like my moves?" Douglas wiggled his eyebrows.

"I've never stopped." They walked in silence for a few moments. "Speaking of moves..."

"Uh-oh."

Gigi laughed. "What? Not us—well, I have no thoughts about moving any time soon, do you?"

"No. Well—"

"Well what? What are you not telling me?"

"Oh, nothing. I was just thinking about some possible travel in our future. We haven't gone anywhere for a while, and maybe there are some trips we'd like to take. I know I wouldn't mind taking my wife on a little adventure."

"Oh, well, that I think could be arranged. I'd go on an adventure with you any day."

"Is that so? One of us does have a pretty big birthday coming up soon." Douglas winked at her. "Darling, maybe I'll take you somewhere to celebrate. Would you like that?"

"I would, yes." As much as Gigi loved where they lived, the idea of going off somewhere alone with Douglas for a few days sounded wonderful to her. "I'm pretty sure Lia wants to do some sort of party, but we could work around that, right?"

"Of course we can, my darling." He pointed down the driveway. "It looks like our greeting committee is on their way."

Gigi laughed as Arianna ran toward them and then stopped to catch her breath. She moved in between them both, taking each of their hands, and then turned toward Douglas. "I saw you dancing with Gigi. And I saw you kiss her." She giggled.

"Did you now?" Douglas reached down to tap her on the nose. "Would you like to dance with me, young lady?"

Arianna looked up at him. "I would."

"Well, alright then. Do you mind, Gigi?"

"Not at all, thanks for asking." Gigi grinned as Arianna looked up at her and reached hands around Gigi's waist.

"Thanks for sharing your Douglas with me, Gigi."

Gigi and Douglas both laughed.

"Oh, I think I would only share him with you, Arianna."

"Okay." Arianna looked like she was deep in thought for a few second. "Don't worry, I won't tell the other girls."

Douglas reached down to pick her up, placing one of her

hands in his so that they could waltz their way up the rest of the driveway.

Isabella opened the door laughing just as the three approached. "Is Douglas showing you his dance moves, honey?"

"Oh yes, Douglas is a very good dancer." Arianna gave Douglas a squeeze around the neck and kissed him quickly on the cheek. "You can put me down now, please."

Douglas obliged and Gigi stepped around them to give Isabella a hug. "How are you doing, honey? And how's that lovely boy?"

"I'm great, thanks. Come on in. Lucas is holding him right now, but I'm sure he'd let you have a turn."

"Yes, I suppose I can share now." Lucas grinned at Gigi as she walked into the house.

"Aww, I don't want to infringe on your time. He looks so content sleeping on you."

"I'm actually going to have to get going anyway. Kate and I have a date. I guess you and Lia will have Annie this afternoon? I hope that's really okay—we don't want to impose."

"Oh, yes. Lia and I have something fun planned with the girls—cookie decorating, to be exact. I'm sure Annie will have a good time."

"I want to play with Annie," said Arianna.

"Honey, you're going to go back over with Gigi and Douglas. Daddy and I will come over later, and we're having our big Christmas dinner tonight."

"A special best behavior dinner?"

Isabella laughed. "Yes, that's right. Although I think you do a very good job of being polite at all the dinners."

"I try to, Mommy." Arianna turned toward Gigi and Douglas. "Okay, let's go!"

Everyone laughed and Gigi leaned down to give Samuel a light kiss on the cheek.

"Don't get up. I guess we are on a schedule."

Arianna ran over to give Lucas a quick kiss. "Okay, see you later, guys."

Isabella hugged Gigi and Douglas. "Thanks again. I'll see you all in a little while for dinner."

TWENTY

How many times had Lia stood in the doorway of their dining room with Antonio's arms wrapped around her as she watched her family sitting around the table that had only grown larger over the years? There were too many times to count, all the wonderful memories flooding her as she watched the girls chattering at their own kids' table set up just beside the bigger table.

"Well, it looks like it's finally time to have this big Christmas dinner you've had planned." Antonio's words in her ear made her shiver.

She turned slightly to kiss him on the cheek. "I'm sure it will be well worth the wait—not for the food as much as the company, of course. Just look at Isabella with that baby. She's positively glowing with happiness, isn't she?"

"She is. I must say, I'm surprised that they were so agreeable to coming so soon after she was released from the hospital, but she looks like the picture of health to me."

"That she does." Lia glanced at her phone.

"Don't worry. You go along, I'll keep a lookout at the

door." Antonio kissed her again before patting her on the bottom.

Lia grabbed his hand while laughing. "Okay, but why don't you come on over and give a toast? I'm thinking it's about that time—that we should probably go ahead and start."

"After you, my darling." Antonio followed her to the table, where they took their places at one end. He handed Lia her glass of wine, then picked up his own. "If I could have your attention, everyone, and if we could all raise our glasses..."

Lia smiled as each person around the table lifted a glass, including the children with their sparkling cider. Her heart was so full with love for this crazy growing family of theirs. She couldn't imagine anything making her happier than this.

She took Antonio's hand when he reached out for her.

"On this day, I propose a toast to you, our family. You mean everything to Lia and me, and our hearts are always happiest when you are here with us. Thank you all for coming—for extending your stays, for we are always happy to have you for as long as you are able to be here. And a special toast to our little Christmas gift, Samuel Richard. We are so happy to be great-grandparents once again. We love you all! Cheers!"

"Cheers!" Everyone clinked glasses around the table and settled in to start passing the heaping platters of food.

Lia quickly put her phone away after glancing at it one last time. She whispered to Antonio, who excused himself from the table for a moment.

She turned to speak to Jemma, who was sitting next to her. "How are the girls doing, dear? Were they able to speak with Rafael today?"

"No. I've been trying to get a hold of him, but no answer, so either he's on a plane or the silly service is out again. It's been so unreliable the entire time that he's been there. I'm trying not to get frustrated with it, but it has been hard."

"Try not to worry. I'm sure he's just as anxious to get back here to you."

"Oh, I know he is. And in a way, with everything being so different here this year—for Christmas, I mean—it's probably not a bad year for him to miss. The girls have been having so much fun together that I don't even think they've realized that Christmas has come and gone."

"Well, then they're going to have a nice surprise when they find out that we're finally opening presents after dinner, aren't they?" Lia laughed.

The kids had opened a few gifts on Christmas Day, but because Lia and Gigi didn't want Isabella or Rafael to miss out, they'd stashed a good portion of the gifts in the closets of the villa. Douglas, dressed as Santa, was planning to appear after dinner with them.

Jemma smiled. "They will. Isabella and I wrote Santa a special note with the girls, telling him that our Christmas was going to be a bit later this year."

"Lia, this veal dish is divine," Gigi said from across the table.

"Chase gets the credit for that one. And yes, it is very delicious. I'm going to have to borrow that recipe for the restaurant."

"My pleasure. I'm happy you all like it," said Chase.

"Who's in charge of dessert?" Kylie grinned. "I can smell something coming from the kitchen."

Chase laughed. "That's gonna be Lia—and Gigi. I was shooed out of the kitchen while they were getting the sugar out. And I missed you in the kitchen today." He winked at his daughter.

"I know. Sorry, Dad. Gabriela needed me," said Kylie.

"Fashion emergency. I'm sure you understand." Gabriela laughed.

Blu reached for Chase's hand under the table. "I'm afraid you're going to have to get used to it, my love. I have the feeling that Kylie is going to be pretty busy in the new year."

On the other side of Chase, Kylie reached her arm up to put it around his shoulder. "Don't worry, Dad. I'll always make time for you."

Chase grinned and leaned down to kiss her on the cheek. "That's my girl."

Lia smiled, enjoying the light banter around the table. "So, while we're all here, we should talk about parties. We've got a big birthday coming up this year."

Kylie and Gabriela looked at one another and grinned.

"Well, if you want to celebrate our seventeenth..." said Gabriela and then looked at Gigi. "But I think you mean Gigi—and her seventieth."

Gigi laughed. "Thanks for outing me, Gabby. I guess there are no secrets around here anyway—especially if Lia is set about a party."

"Gigi, you don't look a day over fifty-nine," said Kylie and everyone laughed.

"So, Gigi's birthday is in April. She and I will talk logistics —about where she wants to have it and all that. I just want to get an idea if an April party will work for everyone."

Lucas looked at his wife, Kate. "Annie will be in school unless it happens to be during her spring break, but we could probably manage to take her out for a few days."

"Yes!" said Annie. "Well, my teachers don't really mind. I do all my homework ahead of time, right Dad?"

"That's right. You do a great job with that, honey. So, yes, I think Kate and I could manage to get away. Just let us know the dates when you know. We never want to miss the chance to be with you all and as always, thank you so much for including us."

"There's no need to thank us for that," said Antonio. "You are family to us and always will be."

"Count us in," said Blu. "We'll adjust our schedules as soon as you know."

"And us." Isabella smiled at Thomas. "And of course, we'll lend a hand where we can."

"Well, I guess I can speak for Raf—" Jemma's eyes went wide and she was out of her seat in a second as they all turned toward a sound in the doorway.

"Rafael!"

TWENTY-ONE

Jemma was weeping uncontrollably as she threw herself into Rafael's arms. "I can't believe you're finally here—standing in front of me."

Rafael took her face with both hands. "I'm so very sorry, Jem. I love you, honey, and I've missed you so much." He kissed her deeply, and Jemma didn't care that they had an audience still sitting around the dining room table.

"Daddy!" Chloe and Daisy ran to hug him.

He finally released Jemma from his arms to grab Chloe and Daisy from where they stood hugging him.

"Hi, girls! Oh, it's good to see you!"

Once Jemma felt at least somewhat recovered, she noticed the two boys, standing back a little behind Rafael as he put the girls back down on the floor.

Rafael put his hand on the shoulder of the tallest boy. "Come, come. Let me introduce you two."

The boys looked a bit taken aback, but they were grinning as they looked around the room at everyone.

"This is Mateo. He's eight." Mateo reached his hand out toward Jemma.

"And this is Nicolas—"

"I'm six." Nicolas also stuck his hand out so that Jemma could shake it.

"Hello, boys. It's so nice to finally meet you." They were still smiling, but Jemma could sense the heaviness in their eyes. Yes, they'd been through a lot—and thank God for Rafael. She felt her eyes already tearing up again as she watched her husband, a protective hand on Nicolas's back.

"It's nice to meet you too. Thank you very much for having us," said Mateo.

Antonio walked over to Rafael to shake his hand, followed by Douglas, who gave him a big hug.

"I bet you guys are hungry, and good for you that you're just in time to share this feast with us," said Antonio. "Would you boys like some dinner?"

Nicolas and Mateo nodded their heads.

Jemma turned toward the twins. "Boys, this is Chloe and Daisy."

"We're four," said Chloe.

Daisy had already tentatively taken Nicolas by the hand. "Do you want to come sit with us at our special table?"

Nicolas nodded his head.

The boys followed the twins to their table and Jemma stood staring at Rafael, her hand still in his, her heart still pounding. She'd never been so happy to see him and now that he was standing in front of her, she didn't want to let him go.

Antonio whispered loud enough for both Jemma and Rafael to hear, "Whenever you're ready to join us." He winked.

"I've got a nice fire going outside, if you'd like to have a few moments alone first."

Rafael nodded. "Yes, I think I'd very much like a few moments alone with my lovely wife. After you, my darling."

Jemma made her way outside to the big overstuffed chairs by the fireplace. She and Rafael had shared many chats in this very place over the years. The night was chilly but the fire gave off plenty of heat.

"Come here, babe." Rafael pulled Jemma out of the chair she was sitting in and onto his lap. "You're too far away from me there and I want you near me—on me." He grinned and finished the kiss they'd began earlier, this time with a passion that made Jemma count the hours before they could retire to their guest house.

She leaned back and looked into his eyes. "I've missed you so much. I can't even begin to tell you how scared I was the day that—"

"Shh." He silenced her with another kiss. "Don't cry. I'm here now—just where I'm meant to be with you—with our family. This last week has been—I don't know—exhausting and emotional and —so many things. But all I could think about was you and getting everything done so that I could come home to you and the girls."

"I know it's been rough. It's terrible—everything you've been through, everything those dear boys have been through."

They were silent for a few moments, Jemma tucked against his chest, feeling the warmth of him, his arms strong around her.

Finally, he put his hand under her chin to lift her eyes toward his. "I'm sorry I missed Christmas. I know I promised you and the girls—"

"Honey, we all missed Christmas this year—well, not really missed it, but we spent it in the waiting room of the hospital, remember?"

"I do remember." Rafael grinned. "You'll have to introduce me to this little Christmas baby." He seemed to be studying her face as he spoke.

Jemma laughed. "What? Does it make me wanna have another?"

Rafael grinned. "I was wondering, that's all."

It was her turn to study his face. "Raf, do you want another?"

"Yes. At some point—I mean, we do, right?"

"Well, I guess that depends."

"On?"

"Well, for one thing, what are your real intentions with these boys, Raf?" Jemma was afraid to ask the question. It was too soon and she'd not even had a chance to get to know them.

Rafael sighed. "The truth is, I don't have an ulterior motive —if that's what you're thinking." He laughed lightly and kissed her on the nose. "I don't know. I just couldn't leave them there —not now. I have them for two weeks, so the plan will be to do a trip back."

Jemma felt her heart lurch. She didn't want him to go away again so soon. It was too soon.

"Honey?"

She looked at him.

"Let's not think about that now." He pulled her to his chest. "Right now, I just want to enjoy being back here with you—having you in my arms. You have no idea how good it feels to hold you like this."

Jemma sighed and let her head rest on his chest again. She

tilted her face just enough to invite another kiss. She couldn't get enough of his lips on hers.

"I love you, honey." He whispered the words as their lips broke for a moment.

"I love you too, Raf. Welcome home."

TWENTY-TWO

Gigi laughed at the sight of Douglas at the door in the Santa costume, perfectly playing the part so well that she was certain none of the children had a clue it was him—not yet anyway. She watched as Arianna, Chloe, and Daisy closed in around him to take his hands and lead him to the living room, where the fire was going in the fireplace and the adults sat drinking their eggnog and laughing at the delighted faces of the children.

The official Christmas dinner that they'd finally enjoyed together had been wonderful and well worth the wait—especially with the surprise arrival of Rafael with the boys. Gigi smiled as she saw Daisy go over to Nicolas, taking his hand to bring him closer to Santa.

The boys spoke only a little bit of English, but there didn't seem to be any communication problems among the children. It was wonderful how easily they'd all taken to one another.

"Ho! Ho! Ho! Gather round, children. I think I'm looking at some kids who have been very good this year."

Gigi went over to where Jemma and Rafael stood whispering to one another. She winked at them. "Don't worry about the boys. I'm pretty sure Santa's got them covered."

Jemma hugged her. "Thanks, Gigi. Things have been so busy lately that I didn't even think about—"

"No need to thank me. And of course, it was Lia too—but you know how much fun we have shopping for the kids. And it was fun to have some little boys to shop for."

"Well, it looks like you did a great job!" Jemma gestured toward the boys, who seemed to be fully into their new electronic games.

"Great! The shop owner assured us that it would be a big hit. And I guess he was right."

She moved a little closer so that she could make out the conversation that was taking place between Arianna and Santa.

"But Santa, how did you know we had a delay for Christmas?" Arianna looked truly puzzled as she seemed to ponder the question.

"Well, don't you remember that letter you left me? On Christmas?" said Santa.

Arianna's face lit up. "Oh yes, I do remember. And we left you cookies and milk."

"Oh, and carrots for your reindeer," Chloe said.

"That's right. I got all the goodies. Thank you very much for that. I'm very busy on Christmas, so I really needed all that energy." Santa put his hands on his belly. "And soon Mrs. Claus is going to want to put me back on a diet again."

Arianna giggled.

"Well, you are a bit round, Santa," said Daisy.

"Daisy!" Chloe shot her sister a look that made both Gigi and Jemma burst out laughing.

"Daisy, that's not polite," Arianna said, putting her arm

around Santa's shoulder. "Don't worry, Santa, that just means there's more of you to love. That's what Mommy tells Daddy about her belly."

Gigi looked over to see Isabella listening in on the conversation and laughing, Thomas's hands around her waist and laughing too as they looked at one another and whispered something that Gigi couldn't hear.

"But Santa..."

"Yes, Arianna?"

"Now I have a brother. He's Sammy. And that means Mommy's tummy isn't so big anymore. Did you know I have a brother, Santa?"

"Ari, Santa knows everything," said Chloe.

"Well, dear, I do know a lot of things, but I don't know everything." He grinned and pulled another wrapped gift out of his bag. "But I do know about baby Sammy—Arianna wrote it to me in her letter—and I was hoping you might like to open his gift for him." Santa handed Arianna a wrapped gift.

"Oh, sure I will. I'd be happy to."

Arianna ripped the paper off of the stuffed animal. "Oh, it's great, Santa! Thank you! It's perfect for Sammy because he's only a baby and soft toys are best. I'm going to go give it to my Mommy to hold for him."

"Okay, honey. Ho! Ho! Ho! Does everyone like their presents?"

"Love it, Santa, thank you so much!" Annie called up from where she seemed mesmerized by her new books.

Gigi laughed because she'd heard Annie whisper to Lucas earlier that she knew Santa was Douglas. "But don't worry, Dad, I won't ruin it for the little kids," she'd said. And Gigi was glad that the books had been a good idea. She'd gotten the series name from Kate, and Annie seemed to be as into it as her mother thought she'd be.

Nicolas gave Santa a hug. Mateo seemed to hold back just a bit but finally followed along beside his brother. "Thank you, Santa."

Both boys said it in unison, and Gigi's eyes teared up as she watched Douglas hug them close. They deserved a home. Gigi was thankful that Rafael had happened to be there for the boys, but there sure was a lot to sort out. She'd been watching Rafael with them all night and she could tell that the boys had already formed a bond with him. She knew that look all too well from her years at the orphanage. Taking them back to Guatemala— probably to the orphanage—was going to be difficult.

Lia came over to stand beside her. "Douglas is so great. I actually can't believe that none of the girls seem to be onto him —well, except for Annie—but the little ones..."

"Oh, he loves it, that's for sure. I'd say we did pretty well with our gift ideas this Christmas—so far."

Lia laughed. "Right. Wait until the kids go back to the other room and discover all the new gifts under the tree. Antonio and I just finished carrying them out from the closet."

Gigi grinned. "Well, this certainly seems to be the Christmas that just keeps on going."

"I say the longer we get to keep everyone here together, the better!" said Lia.

And Gigi couldn't agree more. Everything about the holiday had been perfect, and she wasn't ready for it to end either.

TWENTY-THREE

Isabella laughed and felt Thomas's hands go a bit tighter around her waist as she leaned against him on the sofa where they were sitting watching Arianna with Santa. "Remind me not to say anything in front of that child that I might not want repeated." She shivered as Thomas kissed her on the neck.

"Well, the point remains that your tummy is not near as big now, and I still do and always will love every last square inch of your gorgeous body—extremely large tummy and all—should we choose to grow another one." He winked at her and she sat up a bit on the sofa so she could see his face better.

Before she had a moment to speak, Arianna came running over with Sam's gift from Santa.

"Here, Mommy. It's for Sammy. It's a nice present from Santa, isn't it?"

Isabella reached for her to give her a quick hug. "Oh, he's going to love that one."

"Okay, gotta go back over by the kids and Santa." She turned to look at them once more. "Mommy, Daddy, this is just the best Christmas ever!"

Isabella and Thomas both laughed.

"So, you were saying?" Isabella grinned.

"Well, she is pretty adorable, isn't she?"

"She is, yes. And I think Sammy is pretty sweet as well." Isabella reached over to where their son slept in the portable crib next to the sofa—seemingly oblivious to all the noise going on around him.

Thomas reached for her and pulled her back against him on the sofa again. "Too early to talk about?" He was teasing her, and she grinned back at him.

"Well, you know, seeing how I just delivered our second child less than a week ago, I might want just a moment to catch a breath." She giggled as his hands moved over her thigh. "Thomas, you do realize we're not alone here."

He nuzzled her neck. "Oh, I realize, but everyone's busy watching the kids."

Isabella caught Gigi's eye and smiled as she sat up fully on the sofa, taking one of Thomas's hands in hers. "I'll take a rain check, please."

"That's a deal." Thomas leaned over to kiss her one last time as Isabella caught Jemma's eye and motioned for her to come join them on the sofa.

Isabella hugged her friend, taking in the glow that was evident on her face. "I don't think I even need to ask how happy you are that Rafael is back."

Jemma grinned. "Let's just say that his being here now is pretty much the icing on the cake for what's been a really wonderful week."

"I bet I can make it just a little bit better for you." Isabella winked.

"Oh yeah?"

"Yep. We'll take the kids tonight at our place. The twins can sleep in Ari's room and we'll put the boys in one of the guest rooms. Trust me, I know how much you and Rafael could use a night alone together."

Jemma hugged her. "Thank you for not making me beg." She laughed. "Well, I do appreciate it—and I figured you'd be open to the idea."

Isabella watched the children say their goodbyes to Santa and then huddle together to show one another their gifts. Mateo put his arm around his brother and appeared to be showing him something on his new game.

"I love how Mateo seems to look after Nicolas. It's really very sweet," said Isabella.

Jemma smiled. "I know what you mean. All the kids have been playing so nice together."

"So, have you even had a chance to talk to Rafael about what's happening with them?"

"No—well, only very briefly. He has to take them back in two weeks. I just don't want to think about him leaving again so soon—it's too soon, ya know."

"Of course. Don't worry, Jem. Just enjoy the time you have right now. I feel like the time's gone so fast. I'm not ready for everyone to leave this week. Are you sure you don't want to stay awhile longer?"

"Awww, you know I hate to leave you too. But we'll be back soon. Well, for sure for what sounds like a big birthday bash, but I'm confident we'll get out for at least a long weekend before that. Besides, I'm betting that you two could use some family time of your own—get a good routine going, adjust to life with an infant in the home again." Jemma leaned over to look at Samuel in the crib. "Speaking of—how on earth is he sleeping through all this noise?"

Isabella laughed. "I know. It's good, right? He's actually sleeping really well. Sometimes I have to wake him to nurse."

"Are you kidding? It's fantastic." Jemma leaned back against the sofa just as Rafael came to sit beside her, kissing her on the cheek.

"I think you're pretty fantastic," he said with a wink toward Thomas.

Isabella laughed. "Is that some kinda secret guy code thing you two have going on? Let's butter up the girls and get whatever we want."

"If only it were that easy." Thomas laughed and playfully kissed Isabella on the neck.

Isabella squeezed Thomas's hand and looked toward Jemma and Rafael to her left on the sofa. "I'm having one of those moments, guys." She laughed.

Jemma laughed too. "One of those surreal moments where we look around and feel like we have to pinch ourselves for how lucky we are?"

"Exactly. Lucky in love—and in friendship. I seriously don't know what we would do without you two in our lives. Thanks for being here—for always being there for us." Isabella leaned over to give Jemma a quick hug and had to struggle to keep her sudden emotions in check.

"Well, I would say a big ditto from us," said Jemma.

"Yes, I'd say we're all certainly very fortunate," said Rafael.

Isabella didn't miss the fact that Rafael's gaze was on Nicolas and Mateo playing across the room when he spoke the words.

TWENTY-FOUR

Blu watched the children run to hide while Arianna did her best to count to twenty—something she didn't quite have down yet, but insisted on doing herself, nonetheless. It had been a bright sunny morning, so Blu had all the kids outside while Lia and Gigi worked in the kitchen.

She laughed as she watched Nicolas run across the yard to escape Arianna's tagging him, running only just slightly slower than the small girl so that she could catch him with pride.

"Aww, you got me, Ari!"

Nicolas pretended to pout as Arianna giggled, grabbing his hand so that he could help her capture the rest of the children who were hiding.

Blu grinned as she felt Chase's arms come around her and her head fell back against his chest. She breathed in his clean scent and turned slightly so that her lips nuzzled his neck.

"Don't go."

She wasn't ready to go back to real life. One of the most important things she'd learned from being at the villa the past week was that she and Chase needed to start carving out more time for one another. Their time together had been so precious —even more than usual for some reason—and Blu wasn't ready to give up that magic.

"I know, babe. I'm not ready to go home either." He kissed the top of her head lightly, his lips murmuring his response in her hair.

She lifted her face slightly so that she could look into his eyes. "It's been nice, hasn't it? Our time together here."

He grinned at her. "You can say that again. Kinda reminds me of our early days."

She didn't miss the gleam in his eyes as his arms pulled her tighter to him.

"I know. Me too. Honey, we need to make more time—"

He stopped her with a kiss. "I'm going to do just that."

She looked at him intently. "You are?"

"Yes. Babe, you're too important to me and the time is going by so fast, isn't it? I know I agreed to the whole modeling thing with Kylie, but now all I can think about is the fact that we're each going to be going three different directions, and I don't want that—not that I'm backing out of my support for her, but I just need to be around for more of everything—and especially you, my darling—"

It was her turn to interrupt him with a kiss. It was the perfect way to end their time at the villa together. A shift was coming. They were ready for it. Neither of them needed to work as hard as they did. They certainly didn't need the money. It felt good that somehow they'd seemed to come to the same conclusion without really even having to discuss it.

"I can certainly slow down too." She grinned at him, their lips still nearly touching as she spoke.

"Oh, I'm counting on that." He kissed her and grinned

back at her before giving her one last squeeze. "By the way, those kids sure do look great together, don't they?"

He gestured to where all the kids were now lying on the ground, arms linked in a perfect circle, and Blu could make out that they were chatting about what they could see in the clouds above.

"They sure do. And if I were a betting woman..."

Chase laughed. "Me too, honey. Me too." He kissed her one more time and then let go of her hand that he still held. "Well, I better get on the road. I don't want to interrupt the kids. Hug them for me."

"Okay. I'll see you tonight. Drive carefully."

"Will do. Love you, babe."

"I love you too."

Blu watched Chase until she could no longer see his car after it turned out of the driveway. When she turned her attention back toward the children, she noticed Jemma also watching the kids from the window.

The boys really did seem to fit in well with the whole family. They'd been nothing but lovely, and Blu's heart ached when she thought about everything that they'd been through. How quickly things could change. She certainly knew that in regards to her own life and in fact, in regards to her mother.

Thinking of her now reminded Blu that she owed her mother a phone call. Of course Linda had been invited as usual to celebrate Christmas with them, but she nearly always opted to stay with the children at the orphanage. And Blu missed her.

The thought made her smile. They'd come so far in their relationship. It was true that change was certain, and Blu knew that if she opened her heart to it, she could roll with any changes coming their way.

TWENTY-FIVE

Jemma smiled at she felt Rafael's kiss on her neck and his arms coming around her waist. She could barely put a word to the intense emotion she was feeling, even in her own head.

"They're playing so nicely together, aren't they?" Her words were a whisper as she watched the children from inside at the window. And she felt the tug at her heart that had only grown stronger over the past few days.

Rafael pulled at her gently so that she was facing him as he kissed her on the lips. "Yes. They are, my love."

Jemma tilted her head back slightly so that she could look her husband in the eyes as she spoke. "They're our boys, aren't they, Raf?" She felt her eyes tear up as she spoke the words and just as quickly saw her husband brush away the sudden tears in his own eyes.

"Are you saying what I think you're saying, honey?"

"Yes, but don't act so surprised." She laughed as she leaned forward to kiss him on the nose. "You knew the moment I agreed to them coming here for Christmas. I'm on to you, mister."

"Is that so?" He kissed her deeply on the lips. "Do you have any idea how much I love you?"

"I might have some idea." Jemma laughed.

"We'll need to speak with the girls before we make it official —and the boys, for that matter."

As if on cue, Rafael bent down to lift Daisy up as she ran laughing into his arms, her cheeks rosy from playing outside in the fresh air.

"Can we have some snacks please, Daddy? Outside to share with everyone?"

Jemma leaned over to brush her daughter's hair out of her eyes. "Are you having fun, sweetheart? Do you like playing with the boys?"

Daisy nodded. "So much fun, Mommy." She turned in Rafael's arms. "Daddy, do you have to take them back home? I don't think they are ready to leave, you know."

Jemma caught Rafael's eye and smiled as he whispered to Daisy to go tell the others that snacks were on the way. Yes, just like that, her little family of four had expanded—and somehow even the thought made her feel that much more complete.

She reached for Rafael's hand. "You know this means that we're going to have to move, right?"

The apartment above the garage that Blu and Chase had renovated had been perfect for what had originally been intended as their little family of three. Adding the surprise birth of two babies instead of one had caused a bit of a scramble, but they'd managed to make it work. They had already been looking for a bigger place, news that had Blu feeling better once they assured her that they were hoping to find something in the same neighborhood.

Rafael grinned back at her. "Would you believe that Chase

was just telling me about a very good lead just down the street? He says he knows the current owners and thinks it might be a perfect fit for us."

"Oh, yeah?" Jemma brought Rafael's arm back around her as she nestled in close to his chest and felt his quick kiss along her cheek.

"Yep. Jem?"

"Yes?"

"I'll have to return with the boys next week, and you know it can take a bit of time—the red tape and all. But if we have to, we'll get them settled at the orphanage, so that I can come back here—"

Jemma interrupted him with a full kiss on the lips. "Shh. You're not going anywhere without your family. And those boys aren't going to spend months away from us either. They've been through too much."

Rafael was smiling at her but there was a question on his face.

"We'll all go! It's about time we took the girls there. I'm pretty sure it's just the type of adventure they need—that we all need. And we'll bring our boys back with us." As she spoke the words, her eyes met with Mateo's outside as he waved to her, the grin on his face saying everything.

Rafael squeezed her tight. "Well, I guess that settles it then. Let's talk to the kids." He looked at his watch. "And I think Lia said she'd have lunch ready for one..."

Jemma nodded. Their announcement would be a fun one to share with the rest of the family, and Jemma especially couldn't wait to tell Isabella the news.

TWENTY-SIX

Isabella took a sip of her coffee as she waited for Jemma by the fire. Blu, Gigi, and the older girls had the kids and Samuel over at Isabella's watching a movie so that she and Jemma could steal a few moments alone together before it was time for them to leave. She could hear Lia moving around in the kitchen, likely working on the feast that would be their last lunch together for a while.

Isabella sighed. It was always bittersweet when everyone left after an extended period of time together and there was so much to adjust to, with the addition of a new baby to their lives—a welcome adjustment to be sure. She'd sent her parents home, to come back a week later. A few things had come up for them, and Isabella had assured her mom that a week would be the perfect amount of time—that she would be ready again for their company and their help when they returned.

Annie had cried and cried the day before when it was time for Lucas and family to say goodbye. Isabella had made sure to spend some special time alone with her and the kids, telling her how happy she was that Annie was Arianna's and Sammy's auntie. She would have to make an extra effort to be sure to keep up weekly video chats with her little sister, so that she always knew how important she was to Isabella.

Jemma entered the room with her own cup of coffee and sat down across from Isabella with a big grin.

"Well, you're looking mighty chipper this morning. I take it you and Rafael have been enjoying your reunion week together." Isabella winked, enjoying the funny look on her friend's face. They were so used to teasing one another, and Isabella missed her greatly when she wasn't around. "Oh, Jem, I'm not ready for you to leave today."

"I know. Me either. It's been so relaxing, especially the past few days—and yes, especially my time with Raf."

Isabella didn't miss the blush on her friend's face. She reached her hand out, placing it on Jemma's knee. "I must say that the boys have been so wonderful to have around. Yesterday they were playing so sweetly with Arianna—with her dolls, in fact. It was all I could do to keep myself composed—it was that adorable—but I was careful not to embarrass them." Isabella laughed.

"Oh, I know. The twins love them." Jemma grinned. "Actually that's part of what I wanted to tell you this morning."

"Yes?" Isabella already had a strong suspicion. The writing had been on the wall from the moment Rafael had first spoken to Jemma about the boys and their situation—and Isabella loved them for it. And now Jemma seemed to be too choked up to even say the words out loud.

Isabella handed her a tissue. "Aww, Jem. You're adopting them. I knew it and I think that's amazing. Really."

"You don't think we're crazy?" Jemma laughed lightly through her tears.

"I think you have crazy big hearts." Isabella smiled, feeling choked up herself. "Jem, I think what you're doing is incredible —giving those boys a home, giving them a family."

Jemma nodded. "I mean, I know it might not be easy. I think they're still in a state of shock, to be honest. Well, how could they not be? It's still so soon after losing their mother and grandmother. I'm not even sure that they completely understand what's happened to them."

"Well, you'll be there for them—every step of the way. I think it's wonderful. I'm completely happy for you guys."

"Thanks. I knew you would be." Jemma looked thoughtful. "Isn't it so funny how quickly things can change? I mean, is it just me or does it seem as though it was only yesterday that you and I were traipsing around Europe together?"

Isabella laughed. "Seriously, right? And look at us now— mothers with proper growing families. Wow, it just hit me that you're now going to be a family of six."

Jemma laughed. "Oh, way to freak me out!"

"No, Jem. It's absolutely the best decision. I can feel it. And you're going to be great parents to those boys."

"Yeah, it can't be any other way. When I thought about Rafael taking the boys to the orphanage, it just didn't feel right. I mean, I know that they'd get a lot of care and love there, but I just—I just think they need parents right now. And I guess Rafael probably felt that from the moment he took them in."

"Well, he's a good man. You're a good team, Jem."

The two sat in silence for a few moments, sipping their coffee.

"We're going to go to Guatemala with them next week—the girls and I. We figure that it will be a good experience for them to be at the orphanage, and they're old enough now."

"Good. That makes sense. Do you think it will happen pretty quickly—the adoption?"

"Probably not fast enough, but Rafael seems to think that the process can be sped up a bit—now that they know there aren't any other relatives."

"Well, don't stay gone for too long." Isabella smiled. "It will be quite lonely when you go—not that I don't have good company around here but—there's nothing that compares to having my best friend here. And of course, Arianna is going to miss the twins something fierce. I think she thinks they are living here now. It will be a rude awakening when they have to say goodbye to each other today."

"I know. I'm going to miss you too. That's for sure. It's been really fun having so much time with the girls. We're going to have to get together the moment we get back from Guatemala."

"That's a promise. And on that note, I promised to help Lia set the table. Would you mind giving Blu a call to see how things are going over there? I think Lia wants to be serving lunch at one."

"I'm on it!" Jemma got up from her chair to give Isabella a big hug.

TWENTY-SEVEN

Gigi lifted her drink along with the others sitting around the table. It was their last meal of the Christmas season together. She and Douglas hadn't been home to their place in over a week even though they lived only miles away. It wasn't abnormal really—not when there was so much family staying at Lia's and Antonio's. They used to drive home to their place every night, but then Lia and Antonio had insisted that they should stay in the empty guest house. Gigi had told Douglas that she hated to miss out on any minute of their time together, so it had become the standard now whenever there was family in town.

Rafael and Jemma had just made the exciting announcement that the boys were going to become a permanent part of their family, which had resulted in tears and shouts of celebration. Even the children seemed emotional, having the sweetest celebration at one end of the table. The twins and Arianna had given both boys big hugs, and Gigi didn't think that the pair had looked any happier since their arrival.

Yes, it was a good day and there was much to be grateful for.

Douglas squeezed her knee under the table, which startled her for a moment.

"Hey, mister. Are you getting fresh with me?"

"You know it." He winked. "You looked so deep in thought. I was just wondering what's going on in that beautiful head of yours."

"Oh, nothing really. Just enjoying our last meal together. And the news about the boys. It's wonderful, isn't it?"

"It is, yes. They're good boys and a welcome addition around here. I hope things will go smoothly for them. I spoke with Tori earlier, actually, and she seemed to have a good feeling about it all, so if things go as planned, they should all be back here again in no time."

"That'd be great."

"So, do you think you're ready to get back to sharing some time alone with your boring old man?"

"Please." She leaned over to kiss him, squeezing the hand that was still on her knee. "You're anything but boring or old."

He winked at her. "Well, as long as you think so, that's good enough for me. And I'm looking forward to spending a little time alone with my wife. I've missed that, if I'm being honest."

Gigi laughed at the look that Blu was giving them from across the table.

"You two sure are sweet to one another."

Gigi felt her face grow warm. Douglas was very sweet to her. He always had been, and he hadn't let up on showing his affection over the years.

"Well, I gave up trying to train him years ago. He just can't seem to keep his hands to himself." Gigi laughed and Douglas grinned.

"If only you weren't so alluring, my darling—maybe I'd be

able to." He winked at Blu. "So you all are heading out after we eat?"

"Yep. Rafael has rented a minivan. I suspect he's testing it out as a new vehicle for their suddenly expanded family." Blu laughed. "It's a good thing we finished with the remodel of the guest rooms at our place last month. We'll make do until they find a house."

"Are you taking about us down there?" Jemma said. "We've got our work cut out for us when we get home. The realtor already has several houses to show us—starting tomorrow." She laughed. "Talk about hitting the ground running!"

"Well, let us know if we can help with anything," said Gigi.

"We will—and I do think you two should think about joining us—at the orphanage."

Jemma had mentioned it to Gigi shortly after they'd made their announcement about adopting the boys.

Gigi looked at Douglas and then back at Jemma. "Oh, I think we might need to stay home for a bit ourselves."

Lia and Isabella both looked at her, which made Gigi laugh.

"Oh, don't worry. Not that I won't be coming round here. You can definitely count on me for some baby time—"

"And some Ari time, right, Gigi?"

Arianna's voice right next to Gigi startled her.

"Oh, of course, honey."

Gigi got up to get the glass of water that Arianna was asking her for, and she couldn't help the flash of memory that came. A lifetime ago, she'd had lots of "Ari time" with another little girl called Arianna. One day she'd tell young Ari all about the grandmother that she was named after and how much she reminded Gigi of her namesake.

TWENTY-EIGHT

Lia touched Samuel lightly on the face as she looked down at him. What a sweet addition to their family. He was such a good baby, rarely crying except for when he was hungry or needed a diaper change. She'd be sure to let Bella know that she had plenty of time in her schedule to help her out with the kids, should she need a break.

She watched Bella and Arianna from where they sat across the room at the table. Their heads were bent over some new coloring books that Arianna had gotten for Christmas, and Arianna was giggling as she handed different crayons to her mother.

Bella looked over at Lia. "Is he okay? Do you want me to come take him?"

"No, no, he's sleeping so peacefully." She spoke the words only loud enough for Bella to hear them, not wanting to wake the sleeping baby.

She heard the front door open and close, followed by the voices of Antonio and Thomas. Lia put her finger to her lips as they entered the room and immediately their voices quieted.

Thomas came over to where she sat, kissing her on the cheek, and then seemed to be studying his son's face for a moment.

"Well, this sure is a lovely scene." He smiled at Arianna waving quietly from across the room.

"It's a little quiet." Lia winked.

It had only been a few days since all their guests had left, and Lia was still trying to get used to her and Antonio being on their own again.

"Are you missing everyone?" Thomas asked her.

"I am, yes. I always do. But I like this new normal too."

"And everyone will be back before you know it."

"Yes, in a few months, in fact—for Gigi's birthday—well, depending on where we have the party, I guess. We're going to have to get right on planning that."

Thomas seemed to be studying her as he put a hand gently on her shoulder. "You're really something, Lia. You know that?"

She smiled up at him, the seriousness on his face almost startling her.

"We really love you—and appreciate you so much—both of you," he said as Antonio came over after putting another log on the fire. "I don't know if we tell you enough how much you mean to us—"

"Son..." Antonio pulled Thomas in for a hug. "We love you too."

It was a sweet moment, one that had Lia and Bella across the room wiping at their eyes. Lia so appreciated Thomas's heart and the fact that he was the man that Bella had chosen to be her partner in life.

She reached up to give his hand a squeeze as he bent down to kiss his son on the forehead.

As Thomas made his way over to where Bella and Arianna sat, Antonio sat down beside Lia on the sofa. He leaned over to give her a kiss. "Do you think I could have a turn or is it dangerous to transfer the sleeping baby?" Antonio laughed lightly as he studied Samuel's face.

"Of course you can, Grandpa." Lia carefully placed Samuel in Antonio's arms. "Watch his head now. Do you have him?"

"Yes, my love."

Lia leaned in close to Antonio, her head resting against his arm as they both watched the sleeping baby boy. "He's just an angel, isn't he?"

Antonio nodded and then turned his face toward Lia.

It was that instant—the spark between them as their eyes met even after all these years. It literally made her heart beat faster.

"Are you happy, my love?"

When he asked her the question, she always knew how much he meant it—that he wanted to know her heart in that very moment.

Lia looked around the room—Bella and Thomas laughing at something silly that Arianna had said, baby Samuel sleeping so content in her husband's arms, and Antonio right there beside her—always present, always smiling, and always her best friend.

Her lips brushed against his. "Thank you for the way you love me—and I've never been happier, darling."

And she meant every word.

THE STORY CONTINUES

Birthday Surprise
Legacy Series, Book 12

Available on Amazon

PaulaKayBooks.com

BIRTHDAY SURPRISE — PREVIEW

Chapter 1

Gigi grinned for the photo at Douglas's request, laughing when instead of smiling, he surprised her with a kiss just as he snapped the picture.

"Look, honey, it's the perfect photo of us with the Eiffel Tower in the background."

Gigi took the phone from him to get a closer look. "Well, you've certainly become quite the expert at taking selfies of us, haven't you?" She laughed, handed him the phone, and took his hand to pull him in close to her. "And I don't think I've thanked you near enough for this incredible trip, my darling."

Douglas kissed her. "I've never loved Paris as much as when I've been here with you. Somehow you just make everything that much more exciting and beautiful."

Gigi laughed. "Could it be the fact that I'm your perfect partner in crime when it comes to eating all the crepes in the entire city?"

They'd been to Paris a few times together, but in all their

eighteen years of marriage they'd not ever had a trip as romantic as the past week had been. And Gigi knew how lucky they were.

Douglas laughed too. "Speaking of crepes..."

Gigi laughed. "Sure, let's stop at our favorite place on the way back. I could use a little something sweet."

He kissed her and grabbed her hand. They walked in easy silence for a few minutes, enjoying the sights and sounds around them. What was said about April in Paris was true. It seemed magical to Gigi and she wasn't sure if she was ready for it to end—a bit of a surprise to her, because she was almost always missing their home back in Tuscany whenever they were away.

And she had the party to look forward to. The thought reminded her that she owed Lia a phone call. She checked her phone to reread the last text to her.

"Everything okay?"

"Yeah, I just forgot to call Lia back earlier. I guess I should wait until morning."

"Party planning?"

"Kind of." Gigi laughed lightly. "I must say, I'm quite in the dark about this party—not that I don't think Lia has it all planned and it will be beautiful, but she's definitely being very tight-lipped about it all."

"Well, darling. Maybe they want to surprise you—with some things, I mean."

"Because I love surprises so much?"

"You do love surprises, don't you?"

He was teasing her. She loved it when Douglas surprised her, which was actually quite often.

She leaned over to kiss him on the cheek. "Yes, I do like surprises, I suppose—the good kind, that is."

"Of course—only good surprises for you." Douglas stopped to check his own phone.

"Is something wrong?"

Gigi could always tell when he got a text or email that needed attention. He'd been officially retired for years now, but he still did some consulting and had his hands in a few things back in San Francisco that still needed his attention.

He looked up from his phone. "Oh, no. Nothing's wrong. I just need to make a few calls when we get back to the apartment —after our dessert."

They only had to walk a short distance to the apartment that Douglas had rented for them. It had a balcony and the most perfect view of the Eiffel Tower. The past mornings had been spent sitting together on their balcony, drinking coffee and eating the most exquisite croissants from the nearby bakery. Gigi wasn't at all sure she was ready to leave in just two days.

"So, what's on the agenda for tomorrow?"

"Who has an agenda around here?" He grinned at her.

They traveled well together, both content to not over-plan and to let the days unfold as they did.

"Well, I am meeting Blu for lunch at one. Are you sure you don't want to join us? You're welcome to."

Douglas shook his head. "No, no. You two have your time together. I've got a little bit of work to do anyway, so I'll do it then. How long is she in town for?"

"Just the one night, I think. We've never been in Paris at the same time, so we might also do a bit of shopping."

Douglas laughed. "I knew there would be shopping!"

Gigi laughed too. She rarely shopped for herself, and usually her shopping did involve the expert eye of Blu. It certainly helped to have a fashion designer for a friend, that was for sure.

"Oh, she just has this one shop she wants to take me to. Maybe I'll buy something new for the party."

"That sounds like a lovely idea. Of course you should get yourself a new dress."

They stopped on the corner with their favorite place to buy sweet crepes.

"Chocolate?"

"You know me so well. And promise me you're going to support me going on a diet when we get back." She laughed, but she really could feel that she'd put on a few pounds since they'd been away.

Douglas grabbed her around the waist and kissed her squarely on the mouth. "Nonsense. You're absolutely gorgeous, woman—every inch of you. And of course I'll support you, darling, with whatever you need."

"Well, right now, I need you to hand me a napkin, please, before this chocolate drips all down the front of me." Gigi laughed and followed Douglas to a nearby bench where they sat finishing their desserts.

It was hard to believe that she was turning seventy next week. She certainly didn't feel like a seventy-year-old woman—whatever that was supposed to feel like—and whenever she and Douglas were together, half the time she thought they acted like a couple of teenagers in love.

He grabbed her hand and then rubbed his finger lightly near her mouth, bringing it away with just a dash of chocolate on it—before he kissed her again—almost as if he were reading her mind.

Gigi smiled. If the love and affection of a good man could keep one young at heart, then she didn't think she'd be feeling her age for many years to come.

Chapter 2

Gigi sipped her coffee on the balcony while she waited for Douglas to join her. She loved waking up in Paris, especially with the incredible view from their apartment. Douglas had planned the whole trip as a birthday gift for her and he'd spared no expense to make it the most incredible week they'd ever had together. Gigi would go so far as to say that if they were to choose a second home in Europe, Paris would easily fill that spot for her.

She pulled her sweater a little tighter around her as she leaned forward to peek through the window, where she could see Douglas with his head bent over his laptop. He must have gotten something important during the night, as he rarely did any work before they'd had their morning coffee together. That was true back home as well.

Their morning ritual was easily one of the best parts of Gigi's day. From the day they'd married, they'd never missed a morning coffee together whenever they were physically in the same place.

She closed her eyes as the memories flooded her.

Their first home as man and wife—the home that Arianna had gifted to Gigi—with all the beautiful mornings in the garden—the very same garden where she and Douglas had been married.

And then there had been the countless mornings in Guatemala—the mornings which would start out quiet enough in their small cottage at the orphanage, only to end up surrounded by laughing children.

And then finally, their quaint little villa in Tuscany. It was there that Gigi had felt a full appreciation of this man that she was growing old with—this man who never rushed her in the mornings—or ever, really, for that matter.

Gigi's eyes flew open at the touch on her hand.

"Oh, sorry, darling—and you looked so serene there. Were you resting?" Douglas sat down next to her and lifted the coffee that Gigi had already prepared for him.

"No. I was just remembering." She smiled.

"Oh? Is it a secret then?"

"No, there are no secrets from you, honey. You know better than that." She reached over to squeeze his hand. "I was just thinking about you, actually—how lucky I am."

Douglas brought her hand to his lips. "I'm the lucky one. Everyone knows that."

They grinned at one another, Gigi enjoying the flirtation.

"So, did you get your work done?"

"Yes, yes. Sorry about that. Just one thing I wanted to handle right away. Now, I'm yours for the rest of the morning, dear. And by the way, what a gorgeous sky. Can you believe the colors?"

"The Eiffel Tower looks incredible, doesn't it? Let's be sure to keep all the info for the apartment. I'd like to show it to Blu tomorrow if she has time to come over. I know she has her normal place she likes to stay, but I doubt it could be as divine as this spot you've found."

"Speaking of Blu and Paris, I hear from Chase that she's doing a lot less travel these days—or at least that's the plan once she finishes her current obligations."

Gigi smiled. She'd talked to Blu about the commitment that she and her husband had made to slow down in terms of how much they were working—how much time they were spending apart from one another. She'd fully encouraged her friend, knowing that their marriage would only end up stronger as a result of the decision.

"Yes, and it sounds like Chase already has his replacement at the restaurant. She tells me that they'll both be able to stay all week after the party." Gigi glanced at her phone as it buzzed with an incoming text. "Speaking of the party—that's Lia. I should phone her. Do you mind, honey?"

"No, not all. You go ahead. Take your time, dear."

Gigi took her coffee and her phone from the small patio table and went inside to sit in the comfy corner chair by the fireplace. Lia answered on the second ring.

"Great!"

Gigi laughed. "Good morning to you too. I'm sorry I didn't get back to you yesterday. Somehow the days seem to easily get away from us here."

"As they should, my friend. Are you having a fabulous time? I love the pictures you've been sending us. I've even gone so far as to put a few hints out there to Antonio. It's been ages since we've been to Paris—or really on any type of getaway. I can't wait until—"

"Until?" Gigi grinned as her friend went silent on the other end of the line. "Do you two have some kind of secret holiday planned? Which would be fine, I might add."

Lia laughed. "Oh no, not really. But we should have in the near future. I need to work on getting that man of mine to agree on leaving the vineyard for a long weekend."

"I'm sure Thomas could help—to look after things if you two want to get away. And you should, Lia."

It was ridiculous but Gigi could actually feel her face getting warm. She thought holidays away—for sure in Paris—had to be good for any marriage.

"Well, I certainly didn't want you to call to talk about my nonexistent holiday plans." Lia laughed. "I just wanted to firm up the menu with you. And you do want it outside, yes?"

"Oh yes, it's the perfect time of year for a garden party—well, in your case we have an entire gorgeous vineyard as our backdrop, but your garden is quite beautiful as well."

They chatted for several minutes discussing the party menu and a few other details.

"Well," Lia said, "I certainly can't wait to see you—to see everyone. I know that Bella is really looking forward to it too. Jemma and Blu aren't going to believe how big Sam is already. I swear he's grown even since you saw him a week ago."

"Oh, I can't wait to kiss that gorgeous boy."

By the time Gigi hung up the phone with Lia, she was looking forward to getting back home again—but only after she spent two more glorious days in Paris with her husband.

A NOTE FROM THE AUTHOR

Thank you so much for reading *Christmas in Tuscany*.

If you've fallen in love with these characters and the world of the Legacy Series, I'd love to invite you deeper into the story.

I've written a quiet, emotional prequel titled *Out of Time* that sheds light on the relationships, choices, and moments that shaped everything that follows.

As a thank-you for joining my reader list, you can receive *Out of Time* as a free digital gift, along with future updates and special releases from the Legacy Series and my other women's fiction.

To receive your free prequel, please visit:
PaulaKayBooks.com

I'm so glad you're here.
—Paula

ABOUT THE AUTHOR

Paula Kay writes women's fiction about family, friendship, and the quiet moments that shape who we become.

Her Legacy Series explores love, loss, and the ties that bind us across generations, with settings inspired by Italy, San Francisco, and the places that feel like home long after we've left them behind.

When she's not writing, Paula enjoys meaningful conversations, books that make her cry, and a little too much reality television.

PaulaKayBooks.com

ALSO BY PAULA KAY

Legacy Series:

Book 1: *Buying Time*

Book 2: *In Her Own Time*

Book 3: *Matter of Time*

Book 4: *Taking Time*

Book 5: *Just in Time*

Book 6: *All in Good Time*

Book 7: *Bella's Hope*

Book 8: *Bella's Holiday*

Book 9: *Bella's Heart*

Book 10: *Bella's Home*

Book 11: *Christmas in Tuscany: A Legacy Series Reunion*

Book 12: *Birthday Surprise: A Legacy Series Reunion*

Book 13: *A Summer Together: A Legacy Series Reunion*

Book 14: *In This Moment: A Legacy Series Reunion*

Book 15: *Where It Began: A Legacy Series Reunion*

The Nomadic Sisterhood:

Know by Heart

Stay the Course

Clear the Air

Lost for Words

Out of Touch

Turn the Tide

Rock the Boat

Back on Track

www.ingramcontent.com/pod-product-compliance
Lightning Source LLC
Chambersburg PA
CBHW070040260626
47159CB00005B/2090